O'Brien, Darcy

A way of life, like
any other

DATE			

A Way of Life, Like Any Other

A Way of Life,
Like Any Other

DARCY O'BRIEN

W • W • NORTON & COMPANY • INC •
NEW YORK

Library of Congress Cataloging in Publication Data
O'Brien, Darcy,
  A way of life, like any other.
  I. Title.
PZ4.01288Way   [PS3565.B666]   813'.5'4   77-11093
ISBN 0-393-08798-0

            1 2 3 4 5 6 7 8 9 0

For
THELMA O'BRIEN

Contents

'It's a way of life, like any other.'
—SEAMUS HEANEY,
at the Czech restaurant.

'There's what I want on my tombstone:
Growth, Self-deception, and Loss.'
—BENEDICT KIELY
in Grogan's.

A Way of Life,
Like Any Other

ONE

Casa Fiesta

I would not change the beginning for anything. I had an
electric car, a starched white nanny, a pony, a bed modeled
after that of Napoleon's son, and I was baptized by the Arch-
bishop of the diocese. I wore hats and sucked on a little pipe. I
was the darling of the ranch, pleasing everyone. One day I was
sunning myself in the patio, lying out on the yellow and blue
tiles, contemplating the geraniums and sniffing the hot, clean
air. A bee came up and stung me on my bare fanny. The re-
sponse to my screams was wonderful. Servants everywhere,
my mother giving orders. Don Enrique applied an old Indian
remedy and my father took me down to the beach house to let
the salt water do its work. Oh what a world it was! Was there
ever so pampered an ass as mine?

When my father was away on location, I would go to the
tack room where Don Enrique sat polishing the saddles and the
bridles and the boots and get him to tell me more stories about
my father, how he became an honorary Apache and shot
crocodiles on the Amazon, how he was good to his horses and
courted my mother making *Wrong Romance*. My father said
that Don Enrique's stories were true and wasn't I lucky having
such a wise old man around. Then he would tell me more
stories and I would go to sleep on his big shoulder with my arms
around him.

By the age of five, I could amuse my parents and their friends
after dinner, when they would sit before the great eucalyptus

fire drinking café diablo. Three or four cars would arrive every weekend, and it was a long drive back to Los Angeles, so people would usually stay the night. When conversation livened, my father would send the mariachis away, and I would lie back for a while, absorbing everything and making occasional comments such as 'Is that so?' or 'I hadn't realized that before' until everyone would forget what I was and begin addressing remarks to me:

'They were over budget by a million and a half after two weeks.'

'Is that so?'

'Helen Hayes never got through a second act without dropping half her lines.'

'I hadn't realized that before.'

'You don't know what hell is until you've been a woman directed by Jack Ford.'

'I'd never have guessed that.'

'Louis Calhern's first wife was a great human being.'

'I'll bet she must have been.'

Then Mother would call on me to recite 'The Bishop Orders his Tomb' or 'To a Skylark', depending on the company, and I would go off to bed to applause. One night Charles Laughton asked me would I agree to participate in an experiment with him. He had a theory about Shakespeare, that the rhythms and the music were so perfect and so evocative of sense, that even a child, ignorant of Elizabethan vocabulary, could convey the meaning. He asked me would I read aloud a passage of his choosing. I offered my co-operation, and Laughton called for the plays, which Mother brought, drawing attention to an inscription to her from S. N. Behrman. Laughton let the book fall open, and I found myself working through a speech of Mercutio's, mouthing the syllables and imitating what I took to be good Shakespearean acting style. So attentive was my audience, that I became over-conscious of the sound of my voice, and since I could understand at most one word out of four, I began to fear that the experiment would fail on my account, bringing ridicule to Laughton and earning me his enmity. With a quick movement of my hips I caused the bottoms of my pyjamas to fall to the floor, diverting attention from the text, affording the guests mirth and gaining me a special good-night embrace from Mother and Dad.

These were the Malibu days, the Casa Fiesta days, when I ambled with the ungulates in the chaparral, heard visiting priests celebrate mass in the private chapel to Our Lady of Guadalupe, played with the toys my parents brought me from their travels, the stuffed baby condor from the Andes, the tiny samovar, the voodoo doll, the tortoise shell I used to bathe my puppy in. Whenever they returned from these trips, they had newspaper clippings to show me, so I could see them being received by the Governor of Macao or the Mayor of Panama City. They would bring back some personal memento for me, like a photograph of the Chief of Police of Marseilles, signed: 'C'est avec de sincères regrets que nous apprenons la disparition d'un honorable citoyen de notre ville, ton père, un des plus grands film-stars du monde.' I was too young to accompany them but not too young to appreciate the significance of it all. I often went with my father to rodeos and rode behind him on my pony in the parade and stood beside him when he presented trophies to the winners. There were great banquets afterwards, with steaks so big they drooped over the plates. In San Luis Obispo my father made a speech saying that I was only seven but could already outride half the hands on his ranch. This was untrue, but it earned me a lot of slaps on the back from the cowboys.

One Christmas my father was off making a picture and my mother said she was bored and would take me to New York. She often talked about New York and how much better it was than California, and she said it was time I got out of the provinces and learned a little sophistication. She said I would need proper clothes for the East, so in Beverly Hills she bought

me a gray tweed suit and a camel's hair coat. I looked so elegant.
I spent hours on the Super Chief scrutinizing myself in the
mirror and straightening my tie for my entrance into the
dining car, and by the time we boarded the 20th Century
Limited I felt wholly sophisticated. Mother called me Little
Lord Fauntleroy.

In New York I listened to the radio through most of the days
and nights, and it seemed to me I could have accomplished this
as well in California, but Mother had many old friends from
her years on the stage to see, and she could not be dragging me
about everywhere; but perhaps it was my fault that I did not
do more, because when she took me to matinees I was in-
sufficiently appreciative, falling asleep at the Philharmonic con-
cert in Carnegie Hall and being too free with my opinion of
Giselle, which I called stupid. Mother said she worried what
would become of a boy so insensitive to culture, but it was to
be said for me that I cut a good figure and was well-spoken. At
the hotel, when I was not listening to the radio, I watched snow
falling for the first time, dropped little snowballs gathered from
the windowsill on passers by below, and ordered supplies
from room service as often as I thought seemly.

On Christmas Eve we went to dinner at Lüchow's restaurant
with an old friend of Mother's called Mr Johnny Standfast.

'The Germans have the best Christmases,' Mother said. 'I
never feel it's really Christmas unless I'm at Lüchow's.'

Mr Standfast asked me what I was going to be when I
grew up.

'He'll be an actor over my dead body,' said Mother.

'I think I'll be a diplomat,' I said. I had read about Cordell
Hull in the newspaper.

'You'd make a charming diplomat, dear.'

'I could use a diplomat,' said Mr Standfast. 'I could use a
diplomat right now. I could use a diplomat tomorrow morning. How'd you like to be my diplomat?'

'I never thought of that,' I said.

4

The dinner was the best thing in New York. I said I wished we could eat at Lüchow's every night.

'He's a terrible little snob,' Mother said.

'Is he?' said Mr Standfast.

I praised my mother's appearance. She was beautiful in a navy blue suit with a white collar, her red hair swept up into a pompadour. Mr Standfast said Mother was the most beautiful woman on Broadway.

'That's all finished,' she said. 'To hell with it.' She gave me a glass of wine because I was so grown up in my suit. I liked the wine but it did something peculiar to my eyes.

'You both look very far away,' I said.

When we reached Casa Fiesta my father had returned from location. He wanted to celebrate our reunion with a horseback ride up to Santa Barbara.

'Just like the old padres,' he said. 'El Camino Real. We'll take Don Enrique along and he'll cook Mexican breakfasts on the open fire. *Huevos rancheros. Muy bueno.*'

'I'm exhausted,' Mother said. 'I wasn't able to sleep at all on the train. I think I've a migraine coming on. Besides, you know I detest sleeping on the ground. You go. Big he-man stuff, no, thank you very much. And do take the child, we haven't been apart for a month.'

'Do you want me to call Doc Skaletar?' my father asked.

'I'm perfectly capable of calling him myself.'

So my father, Don Enrique and I set off from Malibu, over the tops of the hills above the sea. From his hat to his boots my father was all in black, just as in his pictures. His horse Tom was black and his saddle black with silver trimmings, his name engraved in silver across the cantleboard. He was a big, powerful man but Tom was big and powerful too and they moved together as one, my father sitting straight with chin out, gazing back and forth across the hills and the sea. He broke the trail, with me second and Don Enrique behind, leading a mule loaded with provisions. We were an outlaw band, we were hunting for gold, we were running down the killers, we were the only survivors of a savage ambush.

We sweated under clear skies, and when we felt like it we turned down to the sea, swam in the icy water and lay on the beach. My father showed me how to get a jump on a wave, swim a few strokes, pull your arms in flat under your body and ride to shore. At night we ate Don Enrique's good food and the two men told stories, and when the sun woke me in the morning breakfast was already cooking. I drank coffee with a lot of milk in it and leapt on my pony feeling like a million dollars.

About noon on the fourth day we rode into Santa Barbara, checked into the Biltmore and took hot showers. The manager of the hotel had worked as a bit player in a couple of my father's pictures.

'*Amigos!* This is a great honor and a great pleasure! And the *senora*, I am sure she is well?'

My father assured the manager that she was well and that she would be sorry not to have seen him, and he introduced me. The manager said it was a great honor to have me as his guest and was I going to be a great cowboy like my father?

'I might try,' I said.

'He's a better man than I am,' said my father. 'You should see him ride the waves. 'He'll be an Olympic champ. But whatever he wants is okay with me. I believe in giving a boy his head.'

The manager and Don Enrique agreed with this.

We had a huge lunch of cold crab on the terrace overlooking the sea, watching the fishing boats and talking of what a swell ride it had been. The men drank lots of Mexican beer.

'This is the life,' my father said.

My father telephoned the ranch and we took a siesta. Then the big green Lincoln arrived and two trucks for the horses and the mule. My father told the driver to put the top down and drive fast. We sang songs all the way to Casa Fiesta.

6

TWO

Growth

But as the hare, whom hounds and horns pursue, pants to the place from which at first she flew, so life turned round on Mother and Dad, and stripped them of their goods and pleasures. It was not the war that did it, but by the end of the war everything had changed. I lived in a house in Los Angeles with my mother.

One night I was awakened by cries from her bedroom. I went in to find her weeping and unclothed, clinging to the bedpost like Christ awaiting the scourge.

'My little man,' she said to me, 'my poor dear little man. Come, see what has happened to me.'

She displayed her wrists, criss-crossed with razor cuts, the blood dried.

'You see,' she said, 'what desperate condition I am in. Save me. *Sauve moi! Comme je suis douloureuse! Mais,* I couldn't do it to you, my poor darling. *Comme tu es jeune!* Too *jeune* to bear it. I couldn't let you see me like that, with blood soaking the damask and in my hair and in pools on the parquet. You can thank me for that, my darling, I love you too much, like a mother.'

I thanked her and asked would she like a glass of water.

'Water? Water? But I've taken so many pills, I shan't be with you much longer. You had better call the doctor.'

I started for the telephone.

'No,' she said, 'no, wait. Sweetheart, don't you know I take sleeping pills every night? Don't you know what I've been through? Poor baby, how could you know? But you must know. Don't call the doctor yet. If you will stay with me, I won't need the doctor. Stay with me and hear my sad story. It is the sad story of a woman.'

I helped her into bed and pulled the covers up to her chin. She had never looked worse, yet she was often so bad that I was uncertain how to act in the present drama. She had lost much of her beauty. Her puffed face was reticulated with frantic capillaries. She kept a bottle close, secreting it behind the salad oil or deep in the folds of her sarong. She sucked on sen-sen and sprayed herself with strong perfume.

'All my life,' she began, 'I have been looking for the perfect man, the perfect love. Is there anything wrong with that? Thank God I'm romantic. I love Roman churches in the winter light, the great ball of lapis lazuli. And all the little cafés. I journeyed up the Nile. I worshipped at Abu Simbel, I have ridden on camelback through the blowing sands of the Sahara. I have stood in the frozen streets of Leningrad wishing on polar stars, rapt before the glories of the Hermitage. Yes, I was disillusioned when they used the same rag to clean the toilet they wiped the tea glasses out with for the samovar on the Trans-Siberian Railway, but I could live with disillusionment, I knew they did that before the Bolsheviks, the Russians have a cruel history, cruelest on the earth, you must read *Anna Karenina*, darling, but I have never found the perfect man.'

I told her that I would always love her. She said that meant more to her than anything in the world. I told her that my father loved her too.

'Your father is a fool, darling, and an idiot. I believed in him once. Oh my God, how I believed in him! He was glamorous. Always the finest tailors. Look at him now, those ridiculous old suits he wears. Hasn't he any pride left? Do you know that he used to put on white cotton gloves and run his fingers over the

8

top of the refrigerator to see that Gerda and Walter, they were the best damned couple we ever had, cleaned it properly? It was the sack for them if they didn't, that was the kind of man he was. Look at him now.'

I resisted speaking ill of my father to her, it seemed a kind of betrayal. But it always made her feel better.

'He's degenerated, all right,' I said.

'He certainly has.'

'He's not the man he was.'

'You're so mature for your age.'

'I don't know what's happened to him.'

'Who would want to stay with *that*?'

'I can't imagine.'

'You're very understanding.'

'What could you be expected to do?'

'God only knows. I reached a point.'

'When did it start happening?'

'There was always a suspicion. But I tried to look for the best. The time he got himself all mosquito-bitten stripped to the waist watching the men put in electricity at the ranch, he looked like such a moron puffed up covered with Calamine lotion, I could have spit in his face. He knew he knew nothing about electricity. He had to pretend. And in South America, the pilots were fabulous, how they maneuvered through the Andes, higher than birds dared fly, it was such a thrill, but your father didn't know the first thing about crocodile hunting, all he wanted was the publicity photographs. The hotel in Rio was crawling with Jewish refugees, but the food was first-rate. I always had suspicions. He has very little hair on his body, did you ever notice that? But he was a wonderful lover in the beginning, I don't think he ever had another woman in his whole life.

'You'll be a man soon. You always were more of a man than your father, God forgive me for saying so, but you reach a point where truth is the most important thing. Hold me, my

9

little man, are my feet growing cold? Always searching, but I have never found the perfect one.'

She raised herself onto her knees, arms flung out.

'Oh God in heaven, God of prayerwheels and the priests in their lovely saffron robes, God of Inca artifacts, God of Bedouins eating figs in tents, God of the Pope in ostrich feathers, Sun God, Moon God, Rain God, God of the seven seas and the lakes with fishes in them, the great whale, the soft rabbit, and I include the snakes and the prairie dogs, God help me find the perfect man. My feet are growing cold, darling. feel my feet.'

They were indeed cold, stiff, and had bad color. I telephoned the doctor as Mother passed from consciousness. The doctor sank a needle into her buttock, shielding me with his body from the sight. She recovered, and no word of the events of that night ever passed between us; and I did not tell my father. But I gave her a bunch of violets, and this note: 'Dear Mother. Please don't die. The bad times will pass. I love you.'

At school I had my own life, which I enjoyed, and I took a certain pride in what help and comfort I could give my mother. I felt that she was coming through a rough passage but that she would make it one day, perhaps by finding her perfect man. Often we would have long talks as she sat in the bathtub, soaping herself and letting water from a sponge fall over her body. Her belly was big now and her breasts droopy, but I was able to imagine her former self and to see how an older man might find her attractive still. The hair on her parts was such a bright red that I had difficulty keeping my eyes from it, but we managed to converse in a lively and civilized way, and there was something about the small, steamy room and the pleasant informality of it all that made possible an intimacy not otherwise easily arrived at. We talked of the joys and sorrows of her life, her hatred of her mother, to whom she had not spoken since the divorce, her favorite composer, Chopin, and of my father, against whom she remained very bitter. We planned dinner parties, the guests, the food and what wine should be served with it. As she toweled and powdered herself, I cleaned out the bathtub, and she would say,

'I wonder how many mothers and sons can talk to each other this way. We're very fortunate.'

The dinner parties were amusing unless Mother allowed herself to get too drunk before they were well under way. I would act as bartender and I would know it as a sign of trouble if she took little drink from me, because that meant she was swilling in the kitchen. Guests praised my highballs and martinis and wondered that a twelve-year-old could attain such skills.

'He's the man of the house,' my mother would say. 'Children should be treated as adults. Make Maggie another bourbon.'

Maggie was a big woman. She often came to dinner. She had a husband, Sterling, who was always recovering from an operation. Maggie had been my father's agent. She had other clients now, and Sterling was in the avocado business. He said it was a good business for him to be in because he was sick a lot, and the avocados more or less took care of themselves. All over America people were eating more avocados. He couldn't get enough of them. They were good for you, much better than a lot of other fruits.

'People should eat two or three avocados a day,' Sterling said. 'The Mexicans understand this better than we do. I always know I'm recovering when I can eat avocados again. I like them plain, maybe with a little lemon juice. Some people like a vinaigrette sauce. There's no better breakfast than an avocado sliced on a piece of whole wheat toast and a cup of coffee. Black coffee, no sugar. People eat too much sugar anyway. It even looks nice, the dark green of the avocado and the black coffee. Sometimes I just look at it for a while before I start. Then there's guacamole, of course. It's going to be the most popular dip in the U.S. in five years' time. Around five o'clock if I'm feeling pretty good, I mix up some guacamole, not too much tabasco sauce, and a pitcher of martinis. It's really nice. I can sit by the pool for hours with plenty of guacamole and a pitcher of martinis. Then maybe half an avocado as a first course. Maggie and I can split one. Sometimes I don't even feel like a second course. Then there's a big firm going to bring out an avocado ice cream. You see, they're such a wonderful fruit you can do anything with them. They make some kind of serum from the pits. I don't know what it cures, but we have a very heavy demand for the pits now. They're such a terrific fruit. People say you can do more things with a tomato, but——'

'Would you shut up with your goddamned avocados!' Maggie would say, and Sterling would be quiet for the rest of the evening, silent in a corner of the couch or at the table, getting up to go to the bathroom three or four times, but moving slowly and carefully, because of his stitches.

We were sitting down to dinner, Maggie and Sterling, Mother and I, and Tony Amalfitano, who ran a camera store in the Farmers Market. Tony was sweet on Mother. He had seen her in the Farmers Market one day and asked if he could take her picture. They had been friends ever since, and he had given me an expensive camera.

'You learn to use that camera yet?' Tony asked me.

'I'm afraid it's too complicated for me,' I said. It was, and I had no interest in taking pictures.

'I don't understand this kid,' Tony said. 'You give him a two-hundred-dollar camera and he won't use it. What does it take?'

'He takes after his father,' Mother said. 'He's no mechanical genius. He won't fix a faucet.'

'He's a intellectual. You like to read books?'

'Sometimes,' I said.

'His father is no intellectual,' Mother said. 'I tried to interest him in the Russian novelists once. Jesus Christ, it was like talking to a tree. Zane Grey was about his speed.'

'I always said he should have been a tuna boat captain,' Maggie said. 'A tuna boat captain. Plenty of fresh air and all those dumb fish.'

'If you mix . . .' Sterling began.

'I've got a terrific part for you, honey,' Maggie said to my mother. 'You're the wife of the mayor of a big city that's invaded by giant insects from outer space. Your husband gets eaten up but you rally the populace and save everybody. There's a love interest, the young scientist who hits on the right insecticide or something. It's a gas. Sam Caliban is directing. He'll wrap it up in three weeks.'

'Sam Caliban,' Mother said. 'He directed me in a picture with Will Rogers. I don't know which of them was more repulsive.'

'Sam never lost money on a picture,' Maggie said.

'Hold it, right there,' Tony said. 'Everybody stop eating. I got to get a couple of shots of this.'

Tony started flashing away. No photo bug could resist that room, the way Mother had decorated it. She had a passion for dining al fresco indoors. The rug was imitation grass and it looked so real that you had to warn people with dogs. The chairs were wrought iron garden chairs and the table was a thick piece of round glass, supported by three plaster columns. There were potted plants around and in a corner on another column a plaster statue of Aphrodite. One night, during an earthquake, Mother had rushed from her bedroom just in time to catch the household goddess, carrying her with hysterical cries safely to the couch, where I found them.

Mother knocked over her wine glass.

'Get a towel,' she said to me. 'Would you, dear?'

In the kitchen I found a bottle of vodka and poured it down the sink. I came back with a towel, and Tony got several shots of me wiping up the mess and pouring salt on the grass. I helped Mother clear the plates and bring out the next course.

Halfway through the Wienerschnitzel, Mother reached

13

across me toward the wine bottle. Her movement was quick and I jerked myself backward in my chair, bringing one hand up to my face, as if to ward off a blow, and grabbing the table with my other hand, to keep from tipping over. Everyone froze, and Mother's face purpled.

'John Agar was around last week,' Maggie said. 'After a part. He looked terrible.'

'My Dad used to give all of us kids a belt,' Tony said. 'Kept us on our toes.'

'My but you're a thick fellow, aren't you, Mr Amalfitano,' Maggie said, and went on to John Agar's drinking problem.

In the kitchen Mother cracked two plates putting them into the sink. We had had a maid but she drank and slept with people on the job, so Mother fired her.

'You little bastard,' Mother said to me. 'Don't you ever do a thing like that again!' She gave me a pretty good slap across the face. 'Embarrassing me in front of my guests!'

Maggie and Sterling left about eleven. As he stepped carefully out the door, Sterling said he would bring those avocados by over the weekend.

Tony fidgeted and poured himself a big Scotch and ginger ale. Mother slumped in a chair, looking unhappy.

'I don't know,' she said. 'Is it worth it? These parties.' Her knees were apart, her sarong falling open.

'You cook great,' Tony said. 'What time you go to bed, kid?' He went over and gave Mother a chivalrous kiss on the top of her head and took a long pull on his drink, replenishing it with Scotch.

The doorbell rang.

'Send them away,' Mother said. 'I don't want to see anybody. I've done enough entertaining.'

'Send them away, kid,' Tony said.

When I saw it was Franz Liszt, cradling a dozen white roses, I knew Mother would want to let him in, so I announced him.

'Oh *wunderbar*!' Mother said. She got up, rearranged her

sarong, and went to the door on tippytoes to kiss Mr Liszt on both sunken cheeks. 'But Franz, darling, what have you done? How beautiful they are! I'll put them in water. I want them to last for the rest of my life.'

'Who is this guy?' Tony said to me.

'A TV director,' I said. In the business, Mr Liszt was known as a perfectionist. His dramatic series had won an award. He kept his people working late, but some gas company, his sponsor, believed in him. He always arrived at our house about midnight, looking as though he had walked from Vienna.

'Franz, this is Mr Amalfitano,' Mother said. 'An old friend.'

Tony stuck out his hand but Mr Liszt walked past him over to the mantelpiece and gestured at a vase of carnations.

'Please to have these removed,' he said. 'They remind me of death.'

Mother told me to throw out the carnations and put Mr Liszt's roses in the vase. Mr Liszt had had a traumatic experience as a youth. His mother had died, and her favorite flower had been carnations. Now he couldn't be in the same room with them.

'I have the champagne, Franz dearest,' Mother said. 'You know I always keep it for you. And shall I put on the Liszt, the Chopin, or the Mendelssohn?'

'Tonight the Liszt,' said Mr Liszt.

I took care of the flowers and the champagne and Mother put on the Liszt piano concerto with a screech of the needle. Tony refused champagne but helped himself to more Scotch. I could see he was uneasy.

'How's business?' I asked him.

'Who'd you say this creep was?' Tony said.

'He's in TV,' I said.

'He looks like he's on it,' Tony said.

'His wife is insane,' I said. 'He spends a fortune on mental hospitals.'

'He ought to join one,' Tony said. 'The guy is a nut case,

obviously. Look at his clothes. He must of got 'em in queers-ville. He come around often?'

'Fairly,' I said. 'Mother says he's very well educated.' She and Mr Liszt were lost in the music, staring at each other. He smoked a cigarette from an ivory holder.

Tony had had enough.

'I'm leaving,' he said. He wanted it to sound like a threat. He drained his drink.

'Franz has the hands of an artist,' Mother said.

I opened the door for Tony. As he went out he grabbed the outside handle and tried to give the door a good bang but I held onto the inside, frustrating him. He stumbled on a step and spent some time fumbling for his key. Mother and Mr Liszt heard him cursing through the music. They came to the window to see him roar off.

'Why do you admit such a class of person?' Mr Liszt said. 'He is beneath you.'

'What can I do?' Mother said. And to me: 'Do you know any Goethe?'

'No,' I said, and excused myself.

THREE

Wrigley Field

The Russian sculptor was only five foot two, but I overheard Maggie say to Mother that he was supposed to be the best lay in Hollywood, much as it was said of a certain actor that he had the biggest dick in Hollywood. I had only an approximate idea of what being the best lay involved, or of what it might involve to Maggie or to Mother, but I knew that Mother considered artists a superior class, on a scale that ran down toward men of independent wealth, Marine colonels, corporation executives, journalists, and retail businessmen, with actors at the bottom. Athletes and manual laborers never entered her mind. I thought her first choice was Mr Liszt, but she determined he was too devoted to his wife. 'Imagine sacrificing your life to a maniac,' she said. 'Not me.' The president of Hillcrest Country Club gave her a car, a television set, and an Amana freezer, but his wife had too much money. Tony Amalfitano hung on as long as he could. At the end Mother refused to answer the telephone, and he would call up at all hours to leave messages with me: 'Tell your mother her tits are no good any more'; 'Tell her I've had better fucks from niggers'; 'Who's getting it tonight? I hope she chokes on it.' She got the police after him, and he left the Farmers Market and went back to New Jersey. Mr Johnny Standfast, whose real name turned out to be Reilly and who had been a handball partner of my father's at the Hollywood Athletic Club, came to stay for a week, but the old magic didn't click. He left with a black eye.

17

The man who invented the Hawaiian shirt ran strong for almost a year. He would fly in from Honolulu and take us to
expensive restaurants. We were going to live on his yacht.
Life would be an endless cruise. Then he began to notice
Mother's drinking, and one morning he had to drive me to
school because she couldn't get up. Mother said she hated the
sun anyway. She had had enough of it with my father.

Maggie brought them together at a party. Mother was to
say later that it was love at first sight. Though he was short, the
Russian stood out in a crowd, a hundred and eighty-five
pounds of east European muscle, a compact rhino of a man. He
made his living constructing mock-ups of animals for Disney,
that was his way of buying time for serious work. Late on the
night of the fateful party, Mother had Maggie telephone me.

'Your mother says she'll be home in the morning and not to
worry.'

'Fine.'

'This is a real bash. Too bad you're not here. What're you
up to?'

'Not much.'

'I'll bet. Just a minute. I'll put Sterling on.'

I listened to the noise, but Sterling never came on, so I
hung up.

The next afternoon Mother told me she had met a great
artist. He was fifty-three years old and had led a cruel life, but
it was not too late for success. He had been wasting his talent in
Hollywood but she was going to try to get him to concentrate
on his own work, which had a perfection, a sense of line and
proportion to it that was not to be believed. The communists
had driven him from his homeland, but he had won a scholarship to an art institute in Brussels. When the money had run
out he had no choice but to sign on with a palm oil trading
company in the Belgian Congo, where he had spent eight
years. The normal tour of duty was four years, after that you
were supposed to lose your marbles from the heat and the

savages, but he was so tough they renewed his contract. He had an indomitable will to live, that was what she admired most about him. He was an artist, but he was incapable of self-pity. You had the feeling that life could do anything to him and he would not say die. She herself was sick to death of weakness. She was ready for strength and beauty, perhaps beauty most of all. He reminded her of a combination of Michelangelo's Moses and David, if it was possible for me to understand that. His aspect was almost Biblical, though he was not a Jew, and he saw deep into life and into her with the instinctive wisdom of the European. There was something to be said for the older civilizations.

Within a month plans were being laid for the wedding. I was flattered and touched that the Russian came to me to ask permission to marry my mother.

'I haf someding vich it is to ask you. I may spik?'

'Of course.'

'How it is I vish to marry your moder, you are de son. In your hands, of course, is it de freedom to make dis act. I haf never am married. I am in loaf wery much your moder. She is beautiful woman, wery kind, smart. She has de vonderful son, vich it is is you. I never haf a son. I would like try be good fader to you. Of course, I can assure you, I haf respek, de great respek your real fader. He is great man, I see him many times de movies. Bot life is strange. A fool can trow it de stone in de wader, and de ten vise men cannot get it out. So?'

I granted my permission immediately. I asked him was it an old Russian custom to ask the son whether you could marry his mother. He replied that since divorce was almost unheard of in his homeland, the matter did not come up, although he had not returned for thirty years and the communists had probably changed things. As he said this, he spat, and I was glad we were in the backyard. In the case of widowhood, he didn't know what the custom was. Asking me had anyway been his own idea.

19

'I think it was very nice of you,' I said.

'So!' he said. 'De bargain it is struck?'

I nodded. He told me to hold out my hand. He slapped it into his, drew me to him, crushed me in an embrace, digging his head into my chest, lifted me over his head like a barbell, and trotted me around the yard in triumph, yelling to my mother that it was time for her to come out. She appeared drink in hand, saying,

'Oh, Anatol, you will be careful with him, won't you?'

He set me down and did a little Georgian dance. Then he had the three of us embrace, and he sang a song, which he said was a sad song about a man who wanders over the globe for many years. At last he returns home. Everyone has died, but he is home, and now he can die in peace. Mother wept.

It was her idea to break the news to my father at a family gathering. She said she saw no reason why everyone couldn't be civilized after so many years of bickering and hatred. Anatol wasn't sure he liked the idea, but he said that when a woman sets her mind to something, to resist it was as foolish as trying to build a wall with your left foot. My father was supposed to take me to a baseball game. When he came to pick me up, Mother would invite him to dinner. I was not to give anything away. When we got back, Anatol would be there.

The Los Angeles Angels and the Hollywood Stars were locked in a tight pennant race and Wrigley Field was jammed to capacity. They had let the overflow crowd stand about twenty deep in the outfield, roped off, and a ball hit into the crowd was an automatic double. My father and I always sat behind the Angels' dugout and we had got to know a few of the players, especially Chuck Connors, a .300 hitting first base-man who was starting a career in movie and TV westerns during the off season. My father would tell Chuck what a won-derful thing it was to be able to hit the long ball and be starting a show business career at the same time, because when your playing days were over you needed that extra insurance to send the kids to college and keep meat on the table. Chuck would tell my father how he used to see his movies every Saturday as a kid in Brooklyn, when the Dodgers were out of town.

We were talking to Chuck during batting practice.

'Hey listen, Chuck,' I said. 'Don't you think it's pretty stupid for the Stars to wear Bermuda shorts?'

'I wouldn't be caught dead in them,' he said. 'On the diamond.'

'They get cut up every time they slide,' I said.

'That's it,' he said. 'Wait a minute.'

Chuck disappeared down into the dugout and came up carrying a first baseman's glove. He gave the glove to me and asked whether I could figure out what was written on it. I made out the words 'SHAD ROE' and the number '29' but I couldn't say what this meant. Chuck told me that the glove had been Preacher Roe's. The Preacher used to fool around at first base and he had given the glove to Chuck several years before, when Chuck had been trying out with the Dodgers during spring training. Now he wanted me to have it.

'Isn't that something?' I said to my father, as Chuck went off to take his swings.

'Just stick with your old Dad,' he said. 'Isn't that right? You can never tell what might turn up.'

I pounded the glove all through the game.

During the seventh inning stretch, while we were standing for the Angels and I was estimating how many Hollywood fans had braved the hostile confines of Wrigley Field, my father asked me why I thought my mother had invited him to dinner. I said I didn't know, but she had said something about wanting everybody to be civilized. He didn't say anything more, and I felt queer not telling him the whole truth, but the game was so exciting that I quickly forgot home troubles. They were tied up 2 and 2 in the bottom of the ninth. I was stomping on peanut shells to ease the tension. Chuck was up with a man on second and two out. He fouled off a couple pitches, and the count ran to 3 and 2. The pitcher, a reliever, threw a lot of knuckleballs, and he was trying to slip a fast ball past, and Chuck lined it into the overflow crowd in right field. He had waited, and he had got his pitch. Perfect timing. You could tell the game was won with the crack of the bat. The crowd stormed onto the field, and the man who had caught the ball, with more sensitivity than your average baseball fan, gave it to Chuck. I couldn't believe it when Chuck came over and gave the ball to me. My father had the presence of mind to ask him to autograph it: 'To my friend and future ballplayer, with best wishes, Chuck Connors.'

'Bizball, I don't understand,' said Anatol. 'De soccer is much faster game. Run run run, all de time. Bizball very slow, I am falling asleep.'

'Soccer is a far superior game,' said Mother. 'Please stop tossing that ball, dear, it makes me nervous. I know how pleased you must be.'

What I really wanted to do was to find a friend and go play over-the-line, but I figured I had better stick around for the big announcement. On the way home from the ballpark my father had said that he hoped maybe my mother had begun to realize what a mistake she had made breaking up the family. They were still married in the eyes of the Church. People made mistakes. The thing was to be able to see your mistakes and not be too proud to confess them. He had made a lot of mistakes in his life, but one thing he had been careful about, he had waited until his thirties to find the woman he wanted to be the mother of his children. A lot of girls had tried to get him to marry them, but he had waited for the right one. Well, you could never predict what would happen in life, but you had to be able to roll with the punches. He wished they had had more children, a big family was the best kind. His mother had eight brothers, so she played shortstop. One of her brothers had gone to sea, another was a doctor, another a priest, they were all successful, and his mother had married his father. He had wanted our family to be like that. He had given my mother everything she wanted. But you couldn't tell about women. My father drove very slowly. It must have taken us an hour and a half to get home. He got lost once, driving up into the Baldwin Hills, but when I told him we were going the wrong way, he said the driving was in his department. I could go anywhere I wanted when I was old enough to drive.

Nothing had been said. Mother kept going into the kitchen to check on the chicken. Anatol was drinking a lot of straight vodka with beer chasers. My father nursed a coke. Conversation dragged.

'*Dîner est servi*,' Mother said.

She was putting food on the plates, slopping bits onto the table, and as she handed my father his portion, she said, very cheerfully,

'Anatol and I are going to be married.'

Absolute silence. Mother finished serving and sat down.

'Well,' she said, 'isn't anybody going to propose a toast?'

Nobody did. Mother started eating, and everyone followed her. Then my father reached over and shook Anatol's hand.

'Congratulations, Anatol,' he said.

My father ate a few more bites. Then he got up from the table, left the room and went out the front door without a word. I went after him.

He was sitting in his car, his hand over his face.

'I'm sorry, Dad,' I said, 'I should have told you. I know I should have. Mother told me not to. It didn't work out.'

He pulled himself together, told me that he loved me, and said I shouldn't have to go through these things. But a man was tested sometimes, and the true test of a man was whether he could get off the floor and still be a champion. I had seen old Chuck out there today. He'd gone o for 3, hadn't he? But when the chips were down.

'You going to mass in the morning?' he asked.

23

'Sure.'

'I'll pick you up,' he said, and he drove off.

The wine was finished and Anatol was struggling with another bottle. Mother was in tears.

'That son of a bitch,' she said. 'He had to go and ruin it, didn't he. He had to make the grand exit. He ruined my life.'

FOUR

Hollywood

I gave my mother away in a Russian Orthodox ceremony. The priest held little crowns over their heads and they were man and wife. Maggie and Sterling were there but they were the only guests, because Mother said she was starting a new life and didn't want all the old assholes around to spoil it.

We moved into Anatol's studio in the Hollywood Hills. There was only one bedroom, so Anatol made me a bed just my size that fit into a corner next to a statue of Syrinx performing fellatio on Pan. He had spent two years on it but had never been able to sell it. My father had wanted me to live with him, but my mother wouldn't hear of it because he was living with her mother. At fourteen I would reach the age of reason under California law and be able to choose between parents, but at thirteen I was happy in my mother's company, content to benefit from her closeness and from such intangible riches as might accrue to me from living in an artistic atmosphere. Also, I knew little of the history, language and culture of the Russian race; not having the means to travel, I was satisfied that by living in the Russian's house, I could observe first-hand his habits, customs, and rituals, and perhaps prevail on him to instruct me in the rudiments of his tongue. I would gain the fruits of a voyage to a distant land, without incurring the cost or inconvenience of transportation.

I was soon to see why Mother thought his art was in need of encouragement. He worked like a devil at it, using every spare hour from his animals at Disney, but in thirty years he had sold only a few pieces, and his studio was therefore difficult to move around in. There were many works in the vein of the Pan and Syrinx statue, mythological figures performing sexual acts of every description. Here, one had to admit, was an imagination of extraordinary fertility and a vision bold enough to couple classical learning with an earthy, contemporary realism. I asked him whether the classical-genital series, begun around 1935 and not yet completed, had a common theme, the grasping of which might help me to bring together in my mind disparate elements of an array bewildering in its complexity.

'De Griks,' he replied, 'dey know it de gods dey are human. You human, me human. You got it penis, I got it penis. What to do wit penis? It is de same problem, de gods and de man. Of course de woman, you know I don't haf tell you. Praxiteles, is all de same. And always de perfection. I try always de perfection. So!'

Anatol was hardly the first Western artist to take as his theme the presence of the human in the divine and the divine in the human, but his genius produced twists and nuances to what in cruder hands could have been dull, cliché-ridden, journeyman's work. His 'Zeus Assaulting Athene', for instance, suggested far more than the obvious quest for union between the principles of creation and knowledge. The work achieved its effect of surprise and antic abandon through a single daring leap in construction: the goddess was five times the size of the tather of the gods, who, captured in the act of scrambling up the female buttocks, reflected in every straining sinew the desperation of a man who may have taken on a task too big for him. 'Will he attain it?' was the question sculpturally posed. And in the eyes, beetle-browed and bulging with determination, lay the answer, 'Yes.' 'I am optimist, in life, in work,' Anatol was fond of saying. The goddess's face conveyed an air of compliance, resignation, with perhaps a hint of gratitude, a sense of chosenness about the mouth. Yet more innovation:

the goddess was clearly a Negress. Some day it would be for the artist's biographer to reveal this subtle link between Anatol's art and his experience as a palm oil trader in the Congo. I told him I understood that such indirect expression of personal life and point of view characterized much twentieth-century art. So he, in effect, was Zeus? 'Dat is de it,' he answered. All life was a struggle. To the victor went the spoils. He had learned a lot from the Belgians.

It was my mother's opinion that Anatol's greatest chance for recognition lay in a chess set he had designed and carved in wood. Each piece represented a portion of human anatomy, the pawns fingers and toes, the bishops ears, and so forth. When you played with this set, the game was an epic of the human body. Since the opposing pieces were distinguishable by sex rather than by color, chess became more a game of love than of geometric position. Mother was certain a big game manufacturer could be interested in the set and that technology would discover a way to mass-produce it. The potential market was limited only by the number of chess players in the world, and by adding an all-male or all-female set to the line, you could take in the homosexuals. 'Faggots love chess, just like anyone else,' she said. You could display it, even if you never played with it. It was the sort of thing that sparked conversation.

I had heard that artists were difficult to live with, and Anatol helped me to appreciate what truth lay in the adage. He made me weed his garden, which had only weeds in it; and when I was blistered and fouled with sweat and dirt, he would summon me to arm-wrestle with him. I would always lose, he had the arms of Haephestos, and like the god his bandy legs gave excellent leverage; but he would say to me, that if one day I could beat him, on that day I should become a man: 'Venn you veaklink beat it me, you man denn!' Afterwards he would challenge me in vodka and beer drinking and in chess playing, which he fell to very vigorously, picking up the pieces swiftly and laying them down with a crack, defeating me always, as I was of a meditative disposition and could not keep pace. Again, I would be a man on the day I beat him. I saw childhood stretching out before me.

He would cook meat in the fireplace, carve it while giving out sharp cries and grunts of pleasure, and dare me to eat as much of it as he. To show his steadiness of nerve, he would pick up my chair with me in it and hold it out at arm's length for ten minutes, meanwhile executing a folk dance to music emanating at tremendous volume from the phonograph. Mother would sit with glazed cheeks and eyes, smiling vaguely, humming to herself, or muttering over and over, 'A real man, a real man.'

Yet I doubt that her happiness with the Russian was ever perfect. Often they quarrelled over each other's drinking. These were pointless contentions, since they were both of them maggoty drunk much of the time, but when it came to counting empty bottles, Mother would win the argument, because she drank and disposed of bottles in secret. They fought about Anatol's friends, whom Mother considered low, and about Mother's friends, before whom Anatol fell asleep. During a particularly troublesome period, Mother took me aside and confided that under the circumstances she was finding it difficult 'to have orgasm.' I had no suggestions to make, but she appreciated my sympathy.

'He's a pig,' she said. 'I think he has Tartar blood.'

'I'm sorry,' I said.

'He's at me day and night. What does he expect?'

'It must be very difficult for you.'

'Difficult! The Whore of Babylon wouldn't put up with it! I don't know, dear, sometimes I think it's all just plain screwing. I don't think there's any love in it. Not that he means harm, the poor thing. I don't think he knows any better. He's had nothing but whores his whole life.'

They had religion in common, and it seemed to give them

some calm. Russian Orthodoxy was but a nuptial diversion. They went to something called the Hollywood Church of Religious Science. I never could make sense of it, but Peggy Lee was a member. Anatol was always getting me to read the literature to him. There was a lot of stuff about people healing ulcers through prayer and how Mary Baker Eddy had been on the right track but failed to appreciate the link between nuclear physics and Revelation and so ended up taking morphine and sleeping in a giant baby buggy. It was Mother's fourth religion. She had begun as a Methodist, turned Catholic to marry my father, then the Russian Orthodox fling, and now this. Anatol said Religious Science had changed his life. He thought I should convert, but I told him Catholicism was enough for me. Besides, I enjoyed going to mass with my father. That and baseball were our only connections then.

One night I was lying in my bed amusing myself with a German nudist magazine Anatol said he used for figure studies, when I heard them shouting and carrying on. Then a noise I later identified as a shoe smashing a mirror, and the sound of Mother sobbing.

'You're a beast, an animal.'

'Shhh! Shad-up lady! You van vake de boy?'

'I don't care. I don't care who knows. What do you know about caring?'

In a little while she emerged with a suitcase. She said she was going to stay at Maggie and Sterling's for a few days. Would I be all right?

Anatol said we should have a party. Mother had been gone for three days and the weekend was coming. He had got over his initial despondency. The night Mother walked out we had stayed up drinking beer and ruminating on the fickleness of women. I had to make it up, since I had had no experience of women, but all Anatol needed was the occasional expression of agreement to keep him going. He told me that the Congolese

29

women were the best, though he had no love for blacks. The
Belgians had everything under control, you could get away
pretty much with what you liked. The Belgians were the best
colonizers. The Belgians and the Portuguese. He had been
much respected in the Congo because of his great strength and
his ability to withstand heat. He had kept a pet leopard that
had loved him like a child. But he had never had a child, except
for any number of mulatto bastards running around the jungle,
but he meant a real child. That was why he was so grateful to
have me now. Did I mind if he thought of me as his son? I told
him I didn't mind in the least, and that I would think of him
always as my father. This declaration cost me some effort. It
made me feel queasy to say it and I took a big swallow of beer
afterwards. But Anatol was touched. He embraced me and,
spreading his arms wide, he said that I should consider the
studio and everything in it my own. That was the first time he
mentioned having a party, and by the time Mother had been
gone three days he talked of little else.

'You know what I mean, party?' he would grin at me.

'Sure, Anatol. I like parties.'

On Saturday afternoon he put two big decanters of vodka
out on the balcony to sit in the sun. They had lemon peel in
them and in a couple of hours they turned yellow. Then he put
them in the ice box with the beer and six bottles of Buena Vista
Green Hungarian wine. He stacked the record changer with
Françoise Hardy and Edith Piaf. I asked him how many people
were coming but he wouldn't tell me. I said I'd be happy to go
out if he wanted to have the party to himself but he said no, the
party was for me. At seven he put a leg of veal on the spit in the
fireplace. He had gone down to the Grand Central Market for
it that morning. He said the Grand Central was the only place
in Los Angeles where he could get a leg of veal the way he
liked it. He was very kind to me all day. He didn't ask me to do
anything, except telephone my mother. She asked me how
Anatol was.

'He misses you,' I said. 'He wants to know when you're coming home.'

'Tell him when I'm good and ready. Maybe never.'

They came about eight, one somewhere in her twenties and the other eighteen, Laverne and Dot.

'You're cute,' Dot said to me. 'How old are you?'

'Fourteen.'

'My brother's fourteen. He goes to L.A. Where do you go?

'I just started Beverly.'

'I hear it's pretty snobby,' Dot said.

'Pretty,' I said. 'I don't know whether I like it yet. Where do you go? You must be in college.'

'I quit school. I hated it. Laverne and I have an apartment. Just off the Strip.'

'Are you two related? You're not sisters or anything.'

'No.'

'How did you meet? Did you know each other before?'

'There's a guy we know,' Dot said.

'You seem older than eighteen to me,' I said.

'You seem much older than fourteen to me,' she said. 'You're very mature. What is this stuff?'

'Vodka with lemon in it. Anatol puts it in the sun. Want some more?'

She held out her glass. I spilled a little on her hand. She licked it off and leaned over and kissed me. I could taste the alcohol in the warmth. I had never kissed a girl before. I could feel her lips, and our teeth touched. My fingers went up to touch her throat. It was so soft and warm. I hadn't thought about anything and it had happened. A thought came to me: this is the most wonderful person I have ever met.

We were sitting very close on the couch. She had one hand on the back of my neck. I could see part way down her dress. It occurred to me that I had never seen breasts before except my mother's and in photographs. I had a pretty good view and I

31

wondered whether she would let me see more, later, or maybe on our second date, maybe at her apartment.

'You want to do it now?' she said.

'See what?' I said.

'I said do you want to do it now.' She hooked two fingers inside my belt.

'Do what?'

'It.'

'We haven't even had dinner.' I looked around for Anatol and Laverne but they had left the room without my noticing. I said I thought I had better set the table. Maybe she would like to look over the statues.

At the table Anatol was in an expansive mood. He kept putting things down Laverne's dress. She was attractive but she had one bad tooth in front. Dot was better. Anatol and Laverne went into the bedroom again after dinner, and Dot and I stood on the balcony and looked at the sea of lights. There was a big traffic jam on the Hollywood Freeway for the Passion Play at the Pilgrimage Theater. I said I would take her to it sometime or to the Hollywood Bowl. She undressed me next to Pan and Syrinx and asked me if I would like her to do that to me. I said sure. She did her best but it was cold-blooded. We were up most of the night. I wasn't anything marvelous but she said I would learn and I probably had a block. I asked her not to tell Laverne, because Laverne would probably tell Anatol, and Dot said she wouldn't, but would I like Laverne to come in too? I said I didn't think that would be a good idea. Dot said she didn't do this all the time. Anatol was paying them seventy-five dollars apiece. There were a lot of guys who took her out. She had been to the Crescendo last week. There was a guy there, a comedian who did a fantastic routine about screwing a chicken. She wanted to be rich so she could go to nightclubs and anywhere she wanted anytime. I told her my father had been a movie star and my mother had been in the movies and on the stage and had made a movie with

32

John Wayne before anybody had heard of him. She hadn't heard of my parents and she didn't believe me, but then she did. She told me I was good looking and would get better looking and should be in the movies myself, and she took hold of me when she said this. I told her a barber had said the same thing to me once, but I had been afraid he was queer because he had kept pressing himself against my arm on the chair. She thought that was pretty funny. There were a lot of fags in her building. Her brother was probably a queer and her father had kicked him out of the house.

In the morning Anatol cooked breakfast and we finished the wine.

'Last night you boy, today you man,' he said to me.

He started fooling around with Laverne, and Dot and I went for a walk. We discussed whether the TV reception was better where she lived. When we got back, Anatol said Mother had telephoned and he sent Dot and Laverne away.

FIVE

Encore Hollywood

To save their marriage, Mother and Anatol decided on a trip to
Europe. At first they were going to save their marriage by
having a child before Mother was no longer capable of it, but
that project broke down when Anatol let out that he would
have to find other women while Mother was pregnant. He had
to put it somewhere, didn't he, and Mother ought to know that
it wouldn't mean anything, since she was the only woman he
loved and the only woman he had ever loved. Then they were
going to adopt a child. Anatol drew up plans for building on a
room, but they couldn't agree whether to adopt an American
child or a foreign one, and the plans were scrapped. They got a
dog, but Anatol ran over it with his car. Mother said the dog
might have made a difference, but she was too brokenhearted
to get another one, at least not right away. They talked to the
minister of the Church of Religious Science, who was a saint,
but he wasn't much help, except that he commissioned Anatol
to do a bust of himself for the foyer of the church. They went
to a marriage counsellor. He put them into a group of similarly
troubled people, but Anatol wouldn't open his mouth in the
group, and after a couple of sessions Mother said she had no
intention of paying good money to discuss her problems with
a bunch of plumbers and Negroes. Anatol started taking tranquilizers, but he didn't stop drinking so he was falling asleep
all the time and he cut out the tranquilizers. He did his work.
Mother sat around, looking tragic and bloated. I tried talking

to her. She said I was lucky to have my whole life before me. As far as she was concerned, life was too damned long. Unfortunately she had a history of longevity in her family. So did my father. He would live to be a hundred. Everyone would live on and on, hating everybody else. Look at her godamned bitch of a mother. Except Anatol would probably drop dead one of these days. His blood pressure was up. He would die and then she would have nothing, except this lousy studio he was too cheap to expand. Didn't she want me to have my own room? Of course she did, but what could she do? She had only enough money left from the divorce to live on herself if Anatol should die. She admitted she had made some bad investments. There was that desert property that never came to anything, that was $150,000 down the toilet. Anatol would die and she would be left with nothing. That was the way it was. Some people gave and everybody else took.

She hit on the trip to Europe during a crisis. At wit's end, she had told Anatol that he had better take her out to dinner. And not one of his cheap dives, either.

'Anyting you vish, Madam,' said Anatol.

'I haven't had a decent dress on for months. Look at me. I was always perfectly chic, and now look at me. You have a great talent, all right. You have a great talent for reducing women to garbage.'

She spent a long time making herself up and getting dressed, and when she came out, I told her she looked beautiful. She thanked me and cried a little, and she told me she was determined to do something to form a more perfect union. She didn't know what it would be yet. At least she was capable of making an effort. She was still able to look like a human being. She was going to make Anatol take her to Scandia and she was really going to let him have it. He couldn't yell at her there.

She got back late, and alone. Anatol had been arrested for drunken driving. She poured herself a drink and sat down to tell me about it. She wasn't upset. She felt rather good, in fact.

She felt better than she had in months, maybe years. They had got to the restaurant, and she had let things alone while they had a few drinks and ordered. Then, during the first course, a lovely shellfish platter they do so exquisitely at Scandia, she had begun letting him have it. She had gone on eating, perfectly at ease, not causing a scene or anything like that, but she had really pulled out all the stops, letting him know what a selfish little bastard he was, how he treated her like dirt, everything. She said she was too damned old to pretend any longer. Well, she had certainly had the desired effect. By the time the main course arrived, veal Oskar for her and tournedos Rossini for him, he was shaking like a leaf and could hardly eat. She had let him order another bottle of wine, that had been her only mistake, but maybe it hadn't been such a mistake after all. She had rendered him absolutely speechless and she had kept it up right through to the pastry cart. Maybe it had been the accent of the waiter or just the general atmosphere, they had managed to get a table in the part that looks just like the Tivoli Gardens in Copenhagen, she had insisted on that, it may have been a premonition, but whatever it was, as they were having their coffee and liqueurs, she had said to him,

' "Darling, darling Anatol. We don't have to go on like this. I still believe in our love, you know that. You know what we must do? We must go to Europe together. Wouldn't it be wonderful? We could see all the places we've never seen together. Don't you have a holiday from Disney coming up?" '

He did, and he agreed on the spot to the trip. I was a little surprised at this, because Anatol had told me that he hated Europe and never wanted to leave America again. He didn't even want to leave California, which he called paradise. Besides, he was fearful of getting too close to the Iron Curtain, because he had the idea that communist agents would be on the lookout for him as an illegal emigrant. They would put him in a camp and torture him and kill him, the way they had the rest of his family. But evidently Mother had been very persuasive.

'Is Anatol in jail now?' I asked.

'They'll let him out in the morning,' said Mother. 'I suppose I'll have to drag down to pick him up. They'll probably take his licence away for a couple of years but that'll be a blessing. We were coming down Sunset. I was making plans, talking about whether to go to Paris or Rome first, and all of a sudden he crossed over the double line and started driving down the wrong side of the street. I screamed "Idiot! Idiot! You'll kill us!" Naturally he panicked and swerved all over the place. I grabbed the wheel and got us over to the side and made him step on the brake. It was a nightmare. A policeman saw the whole thing. Thank God. He was right there in two seconds. I told him to throw the book at him. They asked me to drive him to the station but I told them I had to get home to you. They were nice boys, very sympathetic, so they put Anatol in the squad car. He could hardly walk.'

I was to fly to Paris to meet them for the last week. Mother had said that she didn't want me to miss the opportunity to see Europe but she was sure I understood that she and Anatol would need to be alone together at first to work out their problems and start a new life. Unfortunately she didn't have the money for my fare, so I would have to ask my father. He refused, saying he was broke and was trying to save a little to take me to Bora Bora in a year or so, after they ironed out a TV deal he was working on, but then my mother came on the telephone:

'What do you mean you won't pay for it? For Christ's sake what kind of a father are you? I suppose you want him to sit around this crummy town for the rest of his life with all the bums. Don't you want him to see what culture is? Do you want him to grow up uneducated not knowing anything better than how to shovel horse manure? You're broke, what a laugh that is. I know you've got money stashed away I never knew anything about. You called that a settlement! I don't care if you are broke, you haven't worked in fifteen years, what do you expect? It's not like the old days getting thousands for sitting on your ass on a horse. If I were a man I'd go out and dig ditches just to give my son something. You never go anywhere, you don't drink, you never see anybody or do anything, where the hell do you expect me to believe you spend your money? I wouldn't be a bit surprised if you give it all to the godamned Church. Well let me tell you, you may be able to fool a lot of halfwits but you can't fool me, no sir, I know you too damned well, and if I learned anything living with you all those years it's not to listen to your bullshit. You put that check in the mail today.'

So he came across. Mother said she was glad she was still good for something. If there was one thing she couldn't bear, it was people who cheated their children out of things. And when the time came for me to go to college, I could count on her to be my ally again.

She had wanted to go direct to Vienna to see the opera, but Anatol managed to talk her out of that. He was desperate to keep a buffer zone of at least one country between himself and the K.G.B. He said that going to Vienna was just asking for it. Austria was practically still an occupied satellite. They settled on a week each in London, Rome, Florence, and Paris. She gave me the name of their Paris hotel so I could join them there.

SIX

Paris

At the Georges Cinq, the desk clerk had a letter for me:

Darling little man,
　You know I adore Europe but Anatol has done everything possible to ruin it for me—London was fun, a real honeymoon, but when we got to Rome the trouble started—I didn't get to my age to watch my husband vomit into the fountains at Trastevere—I knew it was the drinking but the prick pretended to be really sick—lying in the hotel room shivering and moaning like a dog—What am I to do—the Pope was marvellous but I've had to do almost everything on my own—the story of my life—Here we are in dear Florence almost a week behind schedule but I am determined to get him to the Uffizi if it's the last thing I do—and to think I have such precious memories of these places—yes dear, some of them even with your father—I trust you arrived safely—now listen, dear, the George V is too big a barn for you to stay in alone you would be utterly lost and besides I understand it's gotten hideously expensive—change the reservation to Friday when we will arrive noon meantime find yourself a decent little pensione or hotel over in the student quarter there are hundreds of them—be sure to find a place where you can take your meals there and I will pay the bill when we arrive—I wouldn't want my only baby to starve to death—just because the monster I'm living with

39

has made things so difficult—try not to run up too ghastly a bill—see you Friday dying to talk to you we will have such fun I know at last—

Your own Mama

I departed the Georges Cinq with regret, but I was able to carry out Mother's instructions. My hotel was small, noisy, dirty but agreeable; the food was good and I was provided a liter of wine a day. I spent my time in the streets looking for women to admire, following them into shops, excited in the trail of their scent. In the Rue St Severin I found Henry Miller's books in the Traveller's Companion Series. These proved excellent bedfellows and spurs to the exploration of the city, but they filled my head with disquieting images. Henry Miller wrote a lot about whores and I gathered that Paris was swarming with them, yet in the streets I saw nothing but healthy-looking people running errands. This was the city of love but I was ill-equipped to find it. My French was rudimentary, I had little hope of engaging a woman in conversation and, could I have found an English-speaker accessible to my purpose, I doubted that I had the aplomb to engineer success. My only sexual encounter, aside from the ritual exhibition of organs in grammar school, had been with Dot, and while this had been instructive, I neither knew where to go to find a whore nor possessed the means to secure her services, if Dot's fee were representative. Comparing prices of bread, cheese, shoes, and books in shops, I found them lower than in California and reasoned that the balance of commerce might favor me in human terms, but I had only 1,000 francs, or about $20, and figured that if Dot had been $75, no Frenchwoman would take less than $50.

Waiting for Mother, I took stock of my life and found it wanting very little. There were other boys my age stuck on farms. In a few years I would be in a position to do almost anything. Heads would turn as I strolled the boulevards and

lounged scanning *Le Monde* in the cafés. There would come a
time when my options would narrow, but I would be ready for
it. In the dining-room of my hotel, I contemplated the American tourists and the French residents and observed that everyone else was worse off than I, old men dining alone, a pair of old
women, American college students boorish in sweatshirts, a
married couple silent, next to me a married couple crotchety. It
would take some effort and shrewdness to navigate through life
avoiding loneliness, boorishness or anger. My father was lonely
and I pondered what mis-steps he had made. Probably he didn't
have enough education, so that when his movie career faltered
he couldn't go right to law school or medical school. That day
in the streets I had seen young lovers. They were appealing.
My parents must have been like that. The trick was to keep
love going. It might work if you gave enough love. Imagine
being forty-five embracing by the Seine.

'They call this coffee?' half the couple next to me said.

'You mail those postcards?' said the other half.

'Sure I mailed them.'

'I want to be sure you mailed them because we're leaving
the day after tomorrow.'

'Why wouldn't I mail them?'

'You might of forgot. You are very forgetful now.'

'If I forgot, so what? I'll mail them tomorrow.'

'Tomorrow is too late. Don't you see? If you mail them
tomorrow we might get home before they do. That wouldn't
be nice.'

'Would you stop?'

'We have to send those postcards, you know we do. You
don't go away and not write. I spent all day on them. They are
the only ways people will know we were really here.'

'If I tell somebody we were here, he will damn well better
believe me.'

'I just know you didn't mail them. Now we'll be home and
people will get the postcards after and it won't be right.'

'Maybe you would like to stop in New York City.'

'What do you mean, you're talking silly.'

'Maybe you would like to stop in New York City, pay thirty dollars a night in some big hotel and stay there so we won't get home before the postcards.'

'I don't want to go to New York City.'

I met Mother and Anatol in the bar at the George Cinq. With them was Peter Pines. He was an ex-actor whom Mother had known in the old days. Now he was working in the Publicity Department for Fox, living in Rome.

'Isn't it too fantastic, darling?' Mother said. 'Peter and I knew each other before Christ. There we were having a drink at the Excelsior and Peter walked up out of the blue.'

'Very glad to meet you, Mr Pines,' I said.

'He has beautiful manners, doesn't he,' Mr Pines said. 'He doesn't look anything like his father. His father was so . . . big.'

'He was big, all right,' Mother said.

'Oh shut up, you,' Mr Pines said. 'Don't be a silly bitch. His father was one of the handsomest men in Hollywood. I'm sure you love your father, don't you?'

'Yes,' I said.

'Peter couldn't resist coming with us,' Mother said. 'Rome is wonderful, of course, but it's not Paris. I wish we had more time. Why did you have to get so damned ill?'

She looked at Anatol and sighed through her teeth. He sat silent, motioning to the waiter for another round. He had vodka and a bottle of beer brought in a silver ice bucket. When he put the bottle to his lips Mother threatened to leave the room. Mother drank Dubonnet and Mr Pines had a perfect Rob Roy with a twist. I took sips from everybody.

'And what have you done with yourself?' Mother said to me. 'Was the Louvre not absolutely beyond description?'

'I didn't go.'

'You didn't go to the Louvre? I suppose you didn't go to the Jeu de Paume either?'

'No.'

'Jesus Christ what a half-wit! Oh brother, that's the last time I'm taking you to Europe. A week in Paris and what did you do?'

'I wandered around. I like it here.'

'I'll bet. Holy God.'

'You should go to Amsterdam,' Mr Pines said to me. He looked me in the eye.

'Why Amsterdam?' said Mother. 'I've never had the slightest desire to go to Amsterdam.'

'You could stick to the Rijksmuseum, dear,' Mr Pines said.

Mother said there was a Russian restaurant off the Etoile that was out of this world. We should go there to cheer Anatol up.

Anatol fell asleep after the blinis and caviar. His glass was still in his hand and Mother took it from him, drained it, and set it down with tragic resignation.

'He looks a bit worn out,' Mr Pines said. 'What have you been doing to him?'

'Let's not talk about it,' Mother said. 'It's too painful. He started having dreams about slave labor camps at the Dorchester. I know how rotten the communists are, but you'd think he could set aside his selfishness just for this trip, wouldn't you? I tell you, Peter, I've never been so glad to see anyone in my whole life. When you walked up, I could have cried.'

'Don't punish yourself,' Mr Pines said. 'Aren't we having a wonderful dinner?'

'It's so sweet of you to put it on your expense account.'

'How do you think I live?'

'I don't know how any of us do. It was one thing when we had money. At least that made living with a bum palatable. But now.'

'You should move to Europe,' Mr Pines said. 'Come to Rome. It's cheaper. You could make wonderful friends.'

'Do you think so? But what about poor Anatol? He has his work.'

'Dump him.'

'I couldn't do that. He'd die without me. He worships me, you see. That's part of the tragedy of the whole thing.'

'You can't throw away your life for a child,' Mr Pines said. 'You're still a beautiful woman. He doesn't deserve you. He's a peasant.'

'His father was a very respectable contractor in Tiflis. He had an audience with the Tsar. The communists slaughtered everyone. Anatol got a scholarship. I believe in his art, I really do.'

'Dump him, sweetheart. Look at him. He's not lovely.'

'You're terribly understanding, Peter, you always were. I'll have to think it over, though. You can't just change your life in two minutes. What do you think, darling?' Mother said to me.

'I don't know,' I said. I was wondering what I would do if Mother went to Rome. I didn't want to live in Rome. I was just getting used to my high school. I was the first freshman ever elected president of the International Statesmen Club and I was a cinch for the boys' honor society.

'You must have some ideas. I've always confided in you. I've treated you like a man. You have a deep understanding, I know you do. Could we have a cognac?'

Mother and Mr Pines thrashed things out over a lot of cognac. Mr Pines said they had a great little colony going in Rome and Mother would be a hit in it. If she needed work he knew someone who could get her a job dubbing Italian pictures. They always needed American voices with experience. I asked Mother whether she still loved Anatol. She said certainly she did, you didn't fall out of love with somebody just because of difficulties, life was complicated under any circumstances, but maybe they were fated to love each other and live apart, there were people like that, it was God's will, that was all she could say. There was no question of Anatol's love for her. He called her his goddess. You had to have a pretty hard heart not to be moved by his devotion, and of course she was moved.

We woke Anatol up and went back to the hotel. I shared a room with Mr Pines as there was little difference in cost from having a room of my own. The bathroom was as big as my room on the Left Bank and I spent a long time in the bathtub looking at myself. When I came to bed Mr Pines was propped up reading the latest *Variety*. He had on silk pyjamas with tiny lions all over them and he was wearing a hairnet.

'Stand there a minute,' he said. 'I think I see a resemblance to your father.'

'I'm tired, Mr Pines.'

'Please call me Peter. It's in the mouth. You have his mouth. He was a very handsome man. You love him, don't you.'

'Every son loves his father,' I said, getting into bed.

'You're very young. It's very hard on you, isn't it? I know. I went through it myself. My father walked out when I was five.'

I closed my eyes. I didn't want to hear about Mr Pines's father. He meant well. We all do.

'I think your mother deserves better than that cretin, don't you?'

'He's all right,' I said. I felt like crying all of a sudden. I turned my face to the wall. Poor Mother was going to be alone again. And poor Anatol, what would he do? Go on at Disney till he dropped? I felt sorry for everybody. What was I going to do? I wished people could stay together. I thought about baseball.

'This is one of the great hotels,' Mr Pines went on. 'I don't know whether I prefer the Ritz, it isn't what it was. The Hassler in Rome is gorgeous. Tony Quinn was in town last week with a new girlfriend. I'll bet you have a lot of girlfriends, do you?'

'Not many.'

'Don't kid me. You're not as big as your father but your face is more sensitive. I'll bet you have a lot of girlfriends. They grow up so fast now, they all look like little whores at fourteen. Wouldn't this be a wonderful place to bring a girlfriend? You could bring her up here and do whatever you liked, couldn't you? Would you like that?'

I didn't answer. I pretended to fall asleep, and I wished he would turn out the light. I heard him unscrew a bottle and take a drink. He sighed a lot. He began a monologue I couldn't follow, something about having children and dying with no one to mourn. When he stopped talking I turned over to look at him. He was wearing a blindfold, asleep, his tongue lying on his lower lip. I put out the light.

That night Anatol raped Mother, or tried to: I am uncertain of his success, I have only her account, and in these cases the shrewdest legal minds have often despaired of definition. This much is certain, that he caused a disruption in the business routine of that hotel and closed forever his avenue of happiness with my mother. I have never seen him since. If he is alive today, I wish for him his health and that after death he may find like Van Gogh the fame denied to him in life.

Mr Pines and I were awakened in the early light by a terrific pounding, as though a body were being hurled again and again against our wall. He, still blindfolded, let out a yell and threw himself into the bedside table, knocking over his bottle, drenching himself with alcohol and cutting himself badly trying to remain upright. I was going to attend to him but I could only rip off his blindfold so he could deal with himself, as the screams in the next room were my Mother's. As I entered the corridor guests were rushing from their rooms, shouting for the bell captain and the gendarmes. With the assistance of a brute anxious to get his hands on the Algerians who had disturbed his sleep, I broke open Mother's door. She and Anatol were struggling at the window. She was resisting his attempts to push her out the window. Had I not arrived at that moment, I doubt that the metal comb with which she was stabbing him vigorously in the chest would have been sufficient to prevent her ejection, for Anatol, bloody but unbowed and like her bare ass naked, had already lifted her up and was moving into his backswing. I slammed into him like a runner breaking up a double play, and my Gallic companion went after him with an awful display of foot work. Other guests crowded into the room and cheered him on to crucify the cochon, and by the time the gendarmes arrived Anatol was unconscious. They took him away. His French, thanks to the Congo, was better than his English, and I hope he was able to explain himself to the satisfaction of French justice, but neither Mother nor I stuck around for the arraignment.

We lunched at Fouquet's. Mr Pines ordered escargots, and I had to dig them out for him because his right hand was bandaged. Mother wore dark glasses and you would never have guessed what had happened except that she slumped because her back had been bruised by the wall. We agreed that she had been very lucky that this had happened with family and friend nearby. Now that it was over she could think about a new life. She would be a long time getting over it but the important thing was not to let it get her down. She would have to try to get Anatol out of her mind, now that he was out of her life. He had been very sweet and understanding, really, when she had begun to tell him that Mr Pines had offered to help her move to Rome and start fresh. She wasn't sure yet, but she certainly thought her life needed a lift. She had devoted herself totally to Anatol, he knew that, but what had he given her in return? Suffering. He blamed his bad European behavior on the K.G.B. and promised things would be different when they got back to Hollywood. He had been nasty about Mr Pines, whom he ought to know was only trying to help a dear old friend from better days, but she was able to understand his resentment. They had started talking about 2 a.m. and had sent for some vodka and beer, but she took very little drink because she wanted her judgment to be crystal clear. The more they talked, the more she became convinced that she should move to Rome and soon. She wondered whether there was any reason for her to go back to Hollywood at all, he could send her things on, she had practically nothing left any more anyway. As her decision hardened, he became erratic, weeping, calling her a goddess, threatening suicide, and abusing her turn and turn about. She was an empress of love, she was a no good slut, she was trying to take me, his son, away from him so she could have me all to herself, she wanted to screw me, there was no one else like her on earth, there were maybe a dozen or a hundred people since the beginning of time with her goodness and capacity to love, she ought to be raped by a company of Cossacks. At dawn he began to see that the game was up. He pitied himself and asked for her pity. Could she not take pity on him one last time? Could she not show him once more that no matter what happened now they had loved each other as no two people had ever loved and had made the most beautiful love together on occasions too numerous to number? He had then had the barbarous impertinence to give himself an erection and to display it to her, straight as a flagpole, as though that of all things would impress her. She happened to have a mouthful of vodka at the moment, and she spat at him, hitting the bulls-eye of his offending member. It was then he drove at her. We knew the rest.

SEVEN

Brentwood

With Mother in Rome I had several choices open to me. Luckily I failed to see any advantage in a Continental adolescence, because Mother wanted to be alone for a while to get her life straightened out. Like any child I preferred living with one parent to living without either, and as my father had become through circumstance something of a stranger to me, I looked forward to getting to know him better. On my return from Paris, I telephoned him and asked whether he would mind my coming to live with him.

'Mind?' he said. 'Son, it's everything I've lived for.'

This made me feel good. But after a few days at his house, I had sized up the situation and decided it was not for me. The problem was my mother's mother. Dad was still living with her, as he had since the divorce. This old donkey had had nothing to do since the Red Cross had ceased making bandages after the Second World War, and caring for my father was her life. Understanding better how to tease the poor creature than to please him, she had become a menace to her charge. His own mother could not care for him, because she had her hands full caring for his brother, my uncle, who had been released from Folsom after serving eight years for embezzling the greater part of my father's fortune. It would not have done to have the two brothers in the same house, they might interfere with one another and fight, though my father was a gentle person who had never done violence to anyone, except in the movies and,

49

if Mother was to be believed, when he had threatened her with a knife over one of her lovers and had struck his fist through a wall behind her head, out of frustration and on account of drink, which he never afterwards took.

Now, in the diminished circumstances in which my father found himself, his money almost gone, his wife gone altogether, his motion picture career apparently behind him, with newcomers like Roy Rogers, Gene Autry and William Boyd already established stars, and the prospect of television bewildering, my mother's mother was not the perfect nurse for him. She was a tough, unsentimental plainswoman, who had never worked a day in her life, my father having supported her since his marriage, her daughter before that, her late husband before that: and the sight of this big man, past fifty years of age, cuckolded and abandoned, robbed and jobless, lolling about the house dreaming of old and better times, disgusted her.

She watched him pining and growing fatter and behaving more and more peculiarly. He had fallen into a religious mania, attending mass and taking holy communion every morning, participating in every sort of Church function—novenas, missions, Holy Name Society breakfasts. The Ladies' Altar Society, which arranged flowers, kept the sacramental bread and wine in stock, and laundered the costumes of the Infant of Prague, had made him an honorary member. He twirled the cage at bingo, he raffled automobiles and turkeys. When the parish sedan was broken down or otherwise in use, he chauffered the priests on their errands of mercy. He never missed a funeral. Because of his physique and the glamor that still trailed from him, he was in great demand as a pallbearer.

All this my mother's mother disdained. She was a Methodist of austere stripe and she ridiculed his superstitions, asking did he wish to run for Pope. With childish mischief she would mislay his rosary beads, delighting in his anxiety when he could not finger them. She made coffee with his holy water and, pretending absent-mindedness, told him of it as he drank, making him sick. During the war, he had spent some time in the Navy, hoping to be assigned to John Ford's photographic unit but ending up teaching running, leaping, jumping, ball throwing and boxing to the recruits at San Diego, except for excursions to the Aleutians and the Philippines, where he contracted in turn double pneumonia and jungle rot, though in the Aleutians he claimed to have captured the first Japanese prisoner. The Navy and the Church were the twin props of his existence: had it not been for them, his depression would have got the better of him. He would have died of a broken heart. But my mother's mother was no more sympathetic to the Navy than to the Church.

When she addressed him as Captain, she did so with contempt. Her malice forbade the respect he desired and deserved. So it is, I philosophized, with our closest relations and friends, that we so rarely receive from them what a stranger would offer, for the moment, freely. Dad repeatedly promoted her in rank, yet for this she neither showed nor felt gratitude. She had begun in his house, as he said, as an enlisted woman. Within a month of Mother's desertion she was made Chief Petty Officer, and soon afterwards Chief Engineer and First Mate. Yet her climb in status was accompanied by no improvement in her decorum. She flaunted military discipline, rising and retiring in defiance of the Order of the Day; defacing the labels he so painstakingly affixed to every cupboard, closet, and drawer; taking out the garbage on the windward side of the house; refusing to stand watch, causing many a sleepless night for him; battening down the hatch to her compartment so that it was impossible for him to carry out his inspection rounds; countermanding his orders for provisions; stubbing out the cigar he allowed himself in the Ward Room after dinner. She claimed the prerogatives of age, though she was but fifteen years his senior and, as my father explained to me, the rawest blue jacket knows that in any military unit, age is no warrant to authority and that in the business of defeating an enemy, a Lieutenant Commander of fifty may take orders from a Commander of forty. In this the military was an emblem of society at large, for, as the experience of the race had shown, it was fatal to have the cares of the state entrusted to the senile. Nor was Granny, half blind, deaf and with spittle running down her chin, the proper judge of what was best for the family.

Natural human sympathy might have prompted deference to Dad's rank, but Granny had a hard heart. I often thought that she must have behaved similarly toward my mother, during crucial periods in that misfortunate woman's infancy and childhood and that, if the discoveries of modern science were to be believed, she must accept blame for her daughter's adult unhappiness and that, if there were a hell, the crone would cook in it. But I could see no way to put her in her place. I was an intruder and she resented me and was prepared to resist me tooth and nail. It would take me months or years to climb past her on the ladder of promotion. I was coming aboard as a mere boatswain and she could deal with me pretty much as she wished. She would not retire, it was a matter of waiting for her to die.

Thinking, I confess, more of my own happiness than of what use I might be to my father, I left his house. I was then in my second year of high school, and while I had yet to determine what course I should set for my life, I sensed that something had gone wrong in both my parents' and that I would have to try an independent approach. I had a friend, Jerry Caliban, son of the famous director, and I had often discussed my family with him. Jerry was of the opinion that my parents were meshugginah and that I should come to live with him and his mother and father in their large house in Beverly Hills. They had so much money, Jerry assured me, that I would scarcely dent the budget. His mother got an allowance of $25,000 a year just to go to the races.

Though I departed my father's house with the possibility of moving in with Jerry in mind, it was several days before I could reach that decision. I took a room in a motel near the high school, and after baseball practice I would come home, turn on the television and try to sort things out. I had not heard from Mother, but I imagined her parading the streets of Rome with her new friends, visiting the churches and museums she loved, maybe working at that dubbing job Mr Pines had suggested. Some day I would be watching an Anna Magnani movie and hear my mother's voice. 'Be off with you, Carlo. Have I no pride? I am a woman. You are scum.' Jerry had a terrific car, a yellow Mercury in cherry condition with black leather insides. I liked the idea of riding around Beverly Hills with the radio turned up looking for girls. He was a year older and could give me pointers. He had already suggested spending Easter vacation in Palm Springs. All the girls went there to get a start on their tans. We could case the pools and pick out what we liked. You could really tell what you were getting when you could see them lying there in bathing suits. You asked them whether they wanted a little help with their sun tan oil. He had met a chick there who carried her own supply of condoms. One night at the motel an old movie of my father's came on the television. He was a U.S. Marshall called in to clean up a town in Arizona. The love interest was Virginia Vale, the daughter of a big rancher. When Dad discovers that Virginia Vale's father is giving protection payments to an out-law gang, she refuses to believe it and banishes Dad from her life. But her father is shot by the gang, and as he dies he confesses everything. Mortified and remorseful, she seeks out Dad and finds him helping the local minister put a new roof on the church. At first he won't come down from the roof, but when she shouts that her father has been killed and that she now believes in Dad implicitly, he leaps directly from the roof onto his horse, a stunt that must have entailed great risk to Dad and, indirectly, to me. He shoots down four of the gang personally and escorts the others to the lock-up. Marriage to Miss Vale is implied at the end. I telephoned Dad to tell him I had seen the picture.

'Where are you, son?'

'Staying with friends. I'll let you know the address in a few days. I have to sort things out.'

'It's your life,' he said. 'But I want you to know there's always a bunk for you here and all the chow you can eat.'

'Thanks. Listen, were you really in love with Virginia Vale or just in the picture?'

'Your mother is the only woman I ever loved and I still love her. You do a lot of things when you're an actor. Is she still in Rome?'

'I think so. Did you ever fall in love at all when you kissed girls in pictures?'

'Sometimes I had to turn my leading ladies over my knee. They were pretty headstrong. A filly can sometimes be more trouble than she's worth. Your grandmother wants to speak to you.'

'I have to get off. Tell her hello.'

I made my decision after the initiation ceremony of the boys' honor society. Jerry was president and he administered the oath with a Bible. I swore to uphold the traditions of the society, not to smoke or drink, and to lead in all ways a life that would set a good example for my fellow students who were not fortunate enough to be chosen members of the society. The sponsor of the society was an old chemistry teacher we called Doc who was notorious for upsetting the girls in his class by making salacious remarks. Doc had recently been a big hit as a contestant on Groucho Marx's television quiz show, and he had signed a contract to do his own show on a local channel. We thought it was great having a celebrity as our sponsor. Doc took me aside and told me confidentially that he was especially glad to have me as a member. He had been a fan of my father's and he could see I was growing into as fine a man as my father. And there was another reason he was glad I had been chosen.

'There are too many Jews in here,' Doc said.

'Is that so?' I said.

'Just look around. Count 'em. There must be eighty per cent Jews. Of course the way this high school has gone the past few years you'd expect that. But I'm glad you're in. We need more balance and leadership. You're Catholic?'

'Yes.'

'That's all right. I'm Presbyterian myself. But we can stick together. I'll help you all I can. I want you to be president some day.'

Jerry took me out for a hamburger later. We talked about how funny Doc was. There was the time he compared the interaction of molecules to a freshman girl on a date with a football star. Jerry wanted to know what Doc had said to me. I told Jerry Doc had said he wanted me to be president some day.

'So do I,' Jerry said. 'I want you to succeed me. Come on, I'll drop you home.'

When Jerry found out I was staying at the motel, he insisted I come home with him. We got my things and Jerry paid the bill. I was grateful because I had no money.

EIGHT

Beverly Hills

The Calibans made me one of their family, and to them, family meant everything. For the first time since Casa Fiesta I knew the warmth and joy of people living together in harmony and trust, and I could hardly believe it when Mr Caliban gave me my own checking account.

'You're gonna live here, you can't come crawling for every nickel,' he said. 'I didn't make it in this business for nothing. I started out sleeping in the back of a shop. Any friend of Jerry's is a friend of mine.'

Sam Caliban ran his house the way he shot his pictures: personally. It was an enormous new house, built to his exact specifications. You entered through double oak doors with brass knockers in the shape of slaves' heads. The living room, which was never used, had velvet furniture in pastel shades and rugs that were gifts from the Shah of Iran. 'The Shah loves my pictures,' Mr Caliban said. 'Nobody knows that. I send him the prints and he sends me the rugs. I could make it as a rug merchant.' The walls were bare except that over the six foot fireplace hung a huge oil portrait of Mrs Caliban dressed the way she was when Sam had discovered her singing ballads in Chicago twenty years before. But the real sitting room was in the back, overlooking the pool, and it was designed strictly for comfort and relaxation. 'I bust my balls all day,' Mr Caliban said, 'I got this to come home to. In fifteen minutes I'm a new man. See that? That's my new Picasso. Don't touch it. The paint's still wet.' There were two other

Picassos, a Rouault Christ, two Chagalls, and a Modigliani. Mr Caliban said that looking at the paintings relaxed him and that if people stopped going to his movies he could send Jerry to Harvard on the Rouault alone. Art was even better than real estate that way. Around the room were six contour chairs that you could stretch out in and adjust to fit your position. They were battery operated so you didn't wear yourself out getting them just right and they had a vibrating mechanism called Magic Fingers and a rocking-rolling mechanism that simulated shipboard travel. 'Everybody sleeps like a baby on a ship,' Mr Caliban said, 'but with these you don't get sick.' There was a bar that was a scaled down reproduction of the bar in the night-club where the Calibans had met and beside it a set of weights and pulleys, so that if you felt you were putting on too much weight from the booze, you could sweat it out without having to leave the room.

Upstairs, Mr Caliban's bedroom was done in a Genghis Khan motif, all red, black and silver with weapons on the walls and a full set of Mongolian armor standing in a corner. Mr Caliban used the armor to hang his suits on, when he came home from work and changed into his relaxing clothes. Mrs Caliban's bedroom knocked your eyes out. It was entirely chartreuse, the walls, the rug, the bedspread, everything. The bed was a four-poster job and the chartreuse hangings had been made to order by some nuns in France. In each of three corners of the room stood a stuffed bear, Papa Bear, Mama Bear, and Baby Bear. Papa Bear was as tall as the ceiling, Mama Bear about eight feet, and Baby Bear about the size of an average American male human being. These, I learned, were symbolic of Caliban family members, and Mr and Mrs Caliban called each other 'Bear' or sometimes 'Big Bear' and 'Little Bear' out of affection. 'Why, we'll just have to get an-other Baby Bear now you're here, won't we, sweetie?' Mrs Caliban said to me. Sometimes she slept with one of the Bear family.

Dinner was served promptly every evening at seven and was a valued ritual, though it lasted only eight to ten minutes because the Calibans ate so fast. The dinner hour coincided with a recorded broadcast of the day's big race from Santa Anita or Hollywood Park. While Mrs Caliban attended the races every day and would know the results before the broadcast, she relived the event in excited reverie, and all of us were caught up in the passion. As the horses left the parade ring, we would finish off the matzoh ball soup. The balls were the size of your fist and for the first several evenings I am afraid I made a mess of things, but no one noticed or cared. The roast got gobbled up by the time the horses were ready in the starting gate. With 'There they go!' we began dessert, and Mrs Caliban revealed where her money was, shouting 'Come on Ballyhamish!' or 'Take the rail Johnny Longden you bastard!' If her horse was in the race to the last, the final furlong in that dining room resembled the first meal for the Donner Party after six months of shoe leather and cannibalism. Spoons rose from plate to mouth and back and forth again faster and faster down the home stretch, Mrs Caliban rising from her chair, standing on it, screaming 'You can do it! You can do it! Use the whip! Go baby go go go!' and then, win or lose, rushing from the room to collapse on a contour chair, giving herself up to the Magic Fingers and calling for an Alka-Selzer. We would join her there and go over what went wrong or right. She did fairly well, keeping careful account and rarely exceeding her allowance in a given year.

Mrs Caliban was a remarkable woman. She was over fifty yet from a distance looked younger than my mother: it was only when you got within three or four feet of her that you could see where she had had her skin tucked up, and her hair was the color of an October persimmon. Like Elizabeth Taylor she had converted to Judaism to marry the dynamo man of her dreams. She had never faltered in her devotion to Sam Caliban: he and the horses were her life. She and Jerry, while not as

58

close as my mother and I had been, had a deep understanding. They rarely spoke to one another but she opened a new charge account for him every Christmas, and while he did resent her in an obscure way I suppose common to most sons, in his heart he wished her well. Once during my tenure she got angry at him for dumping trash into the swimming pool. Jerry argued that the pool man was coming the next day and would take care of it, but she threatened to close Jerry's account at Saks. When she left for Santa Anita, Jerry took an eighth-century battleaxe from his father's room and went to work on Mrs Caliban's favorite contour chair. 'I'll show her trash,' he said. In minutes he had hacked the chair to bits. He deposited the remains in various neighbors' garbage bins up and down the alley and said he couldn't wait to see what would happen. That night, when the big race was over, Mrs Caliban hurried from the dining room. She had lost a bundle and needed that chair badly. She came back to the dining room flushed and sweaty.

'Sam! How many contour chairs have we got?'

'I don't know, Little Bear. Six?'

'Don't Bear me at a time like this. There are five chairs in there and mine is gone. Somebody's taken my chair!'

'Wait till I finish my coffee,' Mr Caliban said.

'Stick your coffee!' Mrs Caliban said. 'Somebody's stolen my chair and I need it!'

'Take mine,' Jerry said. 'It works.'

'I don't want yours I want mine! It has the best Magic Fingers and I've got it adjusted just right. There'll never be another one like it!'

We all got up to search for the chair.

'I don't see it could be stolen,' Mr Caliban said. 'The alarm system works perfect. Anybody gets in here a bell goes off at headquarters.' He counted the paintings.

The maid was summoned for questioning. She kept mum though she must have known what had happened. She had been a trusted member of the family for years, so no suspicion

59

fell to her, and she knew Jerry would reward her. When we gave up the search, Mrs Caliban broke down. Mr Caliban helped her to bed and comforted her with Nembutal. Jerry ordered a replacement the next day, but Mrs Caliban said it could never be the same.

Jerry and I had perfect freedom to come and go as we pleased, but I liked the house so much that I stuck around most of the time. I would sit by the pool and contemplate the water or play the slot machines in the pool house. There was a big supply of quarters, so it didn't cost me anything, and if I won I could keep the pot. Ping pong and billiards, a juke box, a bar, a bowling lane, the pool house had everything. It opened onto the pool with sliding glass doors, and on the rear wall, forty feet across, studio artists had executed a magnificent mural, all in silver and aqua. In the center foreground Sam Caliban was depicted sitting in his director's chair, watching a parade of characters from his pictures. From one end of the wall to the other marched masterful images, Martians, monsters of all kinds, ape women riding giant lizards, toads wearing space suits, the abominable hermaphrodite, Pilar the Pygmy Love Goddess, and a series from Mr Caliban's exploitation pictures, teenage drug freaks, beatnik hubcap snatchers, a runaway nun. You could spend an afternoon just taking it all in. I thought how such a display could comfort my father in his decline.

'How is it you never lost money on a picture?' I asked Mr Caliban. We were on our way to Las Vegas for Thanksgiving. Jerry was driving the El Dorado, with his mother beside him and Mr Caliban and me in the back seat.

'First off,' Mr Caliban said, 'I got an instinct for the property. I know what's gonna entertain your average person who goes to see a movie. Why? Because I'm an average guy myself. Maybe a little smarter, maybe I work a little harder, but I think like the man in the street, and I never forgot where I came from. From nowhere. The business is changing. Not too many guys like me left. A lot of these young guys, they got too much education or too much something, I don't know, they all wanna be Tolstoy, you know what I mean? Back when I started, all the big men were like me. Pants pressers, right? So they knew what everybody liked and they all made money. People laugh about Sol Wurtzel. They laugh like about what he said when they came to him with a script *Dante's Inferno*. Sol said, "O.K. Make it. But one thing. Don't open in the summer." Sure it's funny. But don't you know something? Sol Wurtzel was a genius. There wasn't no air conditioning in those days. A lot of these new guys think you can cram a lot of crap down people's throats and call it art and expect people to pay two dollars for the privilege. Me, I make 'em happy. So what's wrong with that? I pay my taxes.'

I remembered what my mother had said about Mr Caliban and Will Rogers. I would have to disagree with her the next time I saw her.

Mr Caliban had the common touch with his family, too, and with him I felt that I could be happy and stay happy. I had not known that I had been unhappy, but there had been nothing like the sense of well-being I experienced when we drew up in front of the Sands and Jack Entratter came out to greet us personally and showed us to our rooms, palatial suites the hotel had financed with a seven million dollar loan from the Teamsters Union Pension Fund. Fresh flowers and free bottles of booze, fruit baskets, bowls of nuts. Frank Sinatra was expecting us at the dinner show.

Mrs Caliban went off to the pool and Jerry and I followed Mr Caliban into the casino. We had a drink with Julie Ziff, the casino manager and a vice president of the Sands, who was upset because his daughter had married a radical who was buying up thousands of dollars worth of merchandise on Mr Ziff's credit cards and selling it and giving the money to underground revolutionary groups. Mr Ziff was a very fat man with spaniel eyes that had spots under them from cortisone treatments. He was known as the most honest man in Las Vegas. His word was gold, everyone trusted him, and he felt betrayed.

'I don't know, Sam,' Mr Ziff said. 'At least the kid could ask me for money direct. I see where he's bought fifteen sofas. Who does he think he's kidding? I think he can use fifteen sofas in a walk-up? Does he take me for some kind of a jerk or what?'

'The kid's a kook,' Mr Caliban said. 'But he is married to your daughter. I don't see you can do nothing.'

'I'm no reactionary,' Mr Ziff said. 'I vote Democratic. I give to the United Negro College thing. But I think my son-in-law's a godamned communist.' He downed a diet cola.

'He'll grow up, Julie,' Mr Caliban said. 'We all got troubles. How's Frank?'

'Great. Number one. Nothing but high rollers in here all week. But he's worried about Sammy. Sammy's into the mob for so much he'll be a hundred before he pays off. Excuse me, will you Sam? I gotta see Gino. Gino's picking up a package for us tomorrow.'

Mr Caliban explained to us that picking up a package meant picking up money owed the hotel by some gambler. A lot of the high rollers gambled on credit, and the hotel would send a courier to pick up the cash payment. Maybe the guy had to juggle his accounts so nobody would notice how much he was taking out. People didn't like to write checks for gambling debts because it looked bad, and the hotels preferred cash for big debts because it was easier to keep their own records that way and keep the Government off their backs. There was no legal way to enforce collection of a gambling debt, not even in Nevada, so sometimes the hotel had to lean on people pretty heavy. Sometimes they had to threaten murder. The hotel wouldn't get involved directly, of course, but they could hire people. I wondered wasn't it all dangerously illegal. Legal, Mr Caliban said, was how you defined it. The Feds had bugged Mr Ziff's private apartment at the hotel. That wasn't legal. That was a violation of Mr Ziff's constitutional rights. Every time Mr Ziff got on an airplane his luggage got lost so the Feds could search it. That wasn't legal either. It was like any business, you didn't get anywhere if you spent too much time worrying about the proprieties. You had to be first and you had to keep moving in the entertainment business, and gambling was entertainment just like anything else. Nobody brought the gamblers in like Sinatra, but if you didn't collect the debts you couldn't pay Sinatra. It was very exciting.

Mr Caliban had come to Las Vegas to gamble but he wouldn't start until after dinner. Jerry explained to me that his father had a system and once he put the system into operation, he couldn't stop until he won big because stopping would foul up the system. I asked Jerry whether his father always won, and Jerry said sometimes. We had a ringside table at the dinner show and when Frank Sinatra entered to wild applause he came over to the edge of the stage and greeted Mr Caliban and shook hands with him.

'Sam, it's good to see you.'

'Great, Frank, great.'

I felt pretty important and I figured a lot of people in the audience were probably wondering who I was. Sinatra broke into 'I've Got You Under My Skin' and he looked a lot at us and smiled at us. Mrs Caliban said there was no question at all that Frank was the greatest. She wondered whether she had worn the right dress. We were sitting so close I could have touched the chorus girls. Sinatra put everyone into a state of elation. When the check came, the head waiter said it was compliments of Mr Ziff, and Mr Caliban gave the head waiter $50 and the waiter $20.

Mrs Caliban played the slot machines for a while and then went to bed. She didn't like to watch her husband gamble but she let him, because that way he let her go racing. Marriage was a give and take proposition. Mr Caliban played craps. After an hour he was wet and had taken off his coat and tie and

63

rolled up his sleeves. The hotel supplied him with free drinks, but he stuck to beer and didn't drink much. At midnight he drank three quick cups of coffee waiting his turn. By one he was $2,500 ahead.

NINE

Las Vegas

Mr Caliban stayed at the craps table all that night and into Thanksgiving Day. How much he was ahead was now a secret between him and the hotel, and we couldn't actually tell whether he was losing, because he gambled on credit and Jerry said his father's credit line at the Sands was $50,000. Mr Caliban's system, if he was behind, involved betting one third of what he was losing, so that he could make up his losses within three throws of the dice if he got a good run or quit before he doubled his losses if he thought his luck had run out. People who tried to make up a loss 100 per cent on one throw were stupid. He had his meals brought to the action and they were all compliments of Mr Ziff, who slept during the day but had left word.

Mrs Caliban, Jerry and I had Thanksgiving dinner without Mr Caliban because he was still busy playing craps and couldn't quit now. His energy amazed me. I could see how a man like that could manage to never lose money on a picture. We went to the dinner show at the Flamingo, where Joe E. Lewis was performing, and Jerry told me how the Flamingo had been Bugsy Siegel's dream and how Bugsy had been rubbed out in Beverly Hills. I also learned how Joe E. Lewis had got his throat cut, lost his voice and become an alcoholic, and how Frank Sinatra was going to play Lewis in *The Joker is Wild* and would put his heart and soul into the role of the singer who becomes a successful nightclub comedian after

getting his throat cut, losing his voice and becoming an alcoholic. Lewis's jokes were about broads, drinking, and the
pathos of life. He said that when you had to hold onto the floor
to keep it from revolving, you were really drunk. I had turkey
and cranberry sauce because I was feeling traditional, but Jerry
and his mother ate big steaks. The check was compliments of
the management.

We had a fine Thanksgiving, though Mrs Caliban got sick
from the food or the champagne and we had to help her to her
room. Jerry and I went down to watch Mr Caliban, but he
asked us to go away because we interfered with his concentration. He gave us a $100 bill to amuse ourselves with, and we
went to a couple of nude shows, one very elegant where the
girls wore feathers and bared their breasts only from time to
time, the other, in a dive away from the Strip, more direct.
Two attractive girls stuck frankfurters into each other and
then cut them up for bar snacks.

Before we went to sleep, Jerry said he had got the impression
his father was losing heavily, but he warned me not to say
anything about it or ask any questions. This had happened
before, although he couldn't recall his father staying quite
so long at the tables. Mr Caliban had been at it for thirty-one
hours.

We were having a brunch of lox and bagels in the Garden
Room when Mr Caliban came in and said he was ready to go
home. He was still alert, but he was gray, and he slept all the
way to Beverly Hills and didn't wake up till Sunday, after I got
back from mass. My father drove me to and from the church
and we always had breakfast together afterwards, but he never
came into the Calibans. He never asked to come in and I never
asked him to. He was still driving his 1948 DeSoto coupe with
Navajo blankets covering the worn-out seats. It was strange
being with him in the midst of this glamorous life I was
leading. I asked him why he didn't get a new car, and he said
he couldn't afford one. It was better to stick with a faithful old

horse anyway than take a chance on an animal that might shy and throw you where you didn't want to be.

We were in the confessional together, my father on one side and I on the other with the priest in between us. Dad confessed first. I could hear the sound of his voice but I couldn't make out what he was saying, and I wondered what on earth he had to confess. Perhaps he masturbated, that was the only sin I could imagine for him and I doubted even that. It was possible that he wished harm or suffering to come to my mother, but if so he needn't have bothered. I could hear the priest giving him a light penance of a couple of Hail Marys, so he must not have done much. I was the greater sinner, yet he felt more sorrow and guilt than I, it was written on his face. I decided to make a clean breast of things. I told the priest what I had seen in Las Vegas and how it had excited me, and I said that there was a girl in my English class who was making it difficult for me to think about grammar. It was not her fault, but she sat next to me and smelled wonderful and had wonderful legs. The priest asked me how old I was, and when I said I would be sixteen soon he said that I was lucky to be so young, because I had plenty of time to amend my life, yet I couldn't count on an indefinite time because God could call me at any moment. I could be knocked down by a car as I left the church that morning. Or I could get cancer. God's mercy was infinite. He loved all His creatures, from the lowliest caterpillar to the President of the United States. He loved Protestants and he loved Jewish. If I was truly sorry for what I had done and promised to try to lead a good life, I would sit at the right hand of God. I was so lucky to be a Catholic, because I could start a new life that very morning. Wasn't it a beautiful morning? The sun was hot and was drying the dew from the grass. The sun was taking moisture into the air, and one day God would take me into heaven, if I was worthy. It was up to me. If I transferred to Loyola high school, I wouldn't have to worry about the girl in my English class. I should think about that.

Above all I should avoid the occasions of sin. Adam had made us weak, but God's grace could make us strong. My penance was three rosaries and now I was to make a good Act of Contrition.

I borrowed my father's rosary and got through the penance between communion and the last prayers. Dad must have wondered why my penance was bigger than his, but when we were having breakfast at his favorite coffee shop, where he knew the waitresses by their first names, he just asked me whether I was happy. I said I was, and asked him whether he had had a good Thanksgiving. He had taken Granny out to a restaurant run by an old shipmate of his because she needed a rest. Afterwards they watched television. It had been a good Thanksgiving, but he didn't care about holidays so much any more. What had I done? I told him some of it. He said Sam Caliban must be a nice man and I said he was. Families could be great things if they worked right. His father and mother had never been apart. Granny had asked to see me. How about taking a drive down to the beach? We could all use the fresh air on a nice day. I said I had to get back to the Calibans and he said he understood.

Being with my father had depressed me for some reason, and I was glad to get back and take a swim, but when Mr Caliban woke up he got into an argument with Mrs Caliban about how much money he had lost. He refused to say and she said she knew damned well he had gone the limit.

'I don't care what you do with your money,' she said, 'just don't you dare try cutting down my horse allowance. There's going to be a revolution around here, not an evolution, a revolution.'

'Did I say anything?'

'You will. Just try it.'

Jerry and I went into our room to get away from the noise. We lay on our beds watching a football game and Jerry told me about his date with Alice Arbeiter the night before. Alice had the biggest tits at Beverly Hills High. They were so big she had to have a custom made bra. She wasn't very tall and she was skinny everywhere else, so her tits looked even bigger. She had absolutely spectacular jugs. Jerry had been dying to get his hands on them ever since he had first seen her walking across campus in a sweater jiggling to beat the band. It was like they had independent suspension because when she walked one would go up and down and then the other. Well last night he had made it, bare titty from Alice Arbeiter at the drive-in movie. There was a rumor that she was a prude but he had found out different. He had her tits out before the intermission and they were out during the whole second feature. They were even bigger than he had imagined, and they didn't sag at all. He got his hands all over both of them and she went wild when he kissed them. They were so big and full that the light from the movie reflected off them and they probably attracted attention from the other cars. She had actually balanced a coke on one of them. But she wouldn't let him into her pants. Next time. Next time she might just put out all the way.

'Would you ever consider marrying her?' I asked.

'Are you kidding? She failed algebra three times already. Besides, by the time she's twenty-five those things are going to be down to her knees.'

I told Jerry how I felt about Linda in my English class, and he said that Linda went out with guys from U.C.L.A. and was probably humping every one of them. There was a rumor that Linda already had an abortion. I was sorry to hear that but I wanted to date her anyway.

'We should have a double date,' Jerry said. 'Me and Alice and you and Linda.' I thought of what it would be like sitting in the back seat of Jerry's Mercury with my hand all over Linda's thighs watching Jerry handle Alice's enormous garboons in front. That would be something.

Mr Caliban didn't like losing money, and when he did lose he tried to make it up as soon as possible. Mr Ziff was glad to extend his credit, and in the next couple of months he flew to Las Vegas several times to try to win back his money. He wasn't having any luck, and what made it worse, the picture he was working on, a jungle epic, was running into production difficulties and was over budget. It might turn out to be the first picture he ever lost money on, and it couldn't have come at a more inconvenient time. One evening in March we were sitting in the contour chairs waiting for Mr Caliban to get home from the studio. Mrs Caliban answered the telephone.

'No. Sam's not here. I'm expecting him soon. . . . Yes, I can take a message. . . . What's that? . . . Who is this? What're you trying to do, scare me to death?' She listened silently. It must have been very bad news. I wondered whether Mr Caliban had been killed on the freeway. Then she took the receiver away from her ear and stared at it, as people do when the other party has hung up.

'Pour me a gin, Jerry,' she said. 'Make it a double. Oh my God.'

Jerry asked her what had happened but she wouldn't speak. When Mr Caliban came in she rushed to his arms.

'Bear, Bear, Big Bear! What are they trying to do to you? I was afraid you were already dead. Hold me, Bear, I can't live without you.'

'Reports of my death are premature,' Mr Caliban said. 'Mark Twain. What the hell is this?'

'That's what I want to know, Big Bear of my heart. Why do they want to kill you? Who would want to kill the sweetest guy on the face of the earth? Oh sweetest love Bear, they said they'd kill you.'

Mr Caliban made himself a drink and we all got into the chairs. Mrs Caliban said this terrible voice on the phone had threatened to murder her Bear. The voice had said that if he didn't take care of that matter and quick, his life wasn't worth shit. That was what the voice had said.

'It must be a mistake,' Mr Caliban said. 'There must be a

70

thousand Sam Calibans in this godamned country. There's a Sam Caliban in Jersey City. I'll take care of it, Little Bear. Don't you worry. There's a million nuts loose in this country.'

'I can't take this,' Mrs Caliban said. 'I almost died of fright. Is there any Nembutal?'

'Jerry, get your mother a Nembutal. Some bastard is scaring hell out of my wife. I'll take care of it.'

Mr Caliban contemplated a Picasso.

TEN

Palm Springs

Jerry told me his father was having a crisis. His father had a new girl friend, and that was probably at the heart of it. He had had girl friends off and on as long as Jerry could remember, but never anything serious. The new one was taking up too much of his time and was costing him money. He had cast her as the lead in the jungle epic. She had dark, shiny skin, big dark eyes and gorgeous legs, and she had seemed absolutely typecast for the part of the girl who is raised by a cheetah family, but she couldn't act worth a damn. Mr Caliban had tried everything. He had even had her dialogue written out of the script so all she had to do was purr, and that could be dubbed, but she was hopeless. She ruined every scene she was in. So he had demoted her to a supporting role. She was pretty mad about that and he had had to make it up to her in other ways, Cartier rocks and a penthouse on South Rodeo Drive that set him back $500 a month, and he was wasting time and pots of cash keeping her happy. Imagine a man of his age going bananas just to keep his end in.

And on top of her the gambling debts. After the threat Mr Caliban called his friend Ziff. Mr Ziff expressed shock and mortification and said he would get right on it, but it would probably be a good idea if Mr Caliban made an instalment payment on the debt, say $50,000. That would make it easier for Mr Ziff to handle the hot-heads in the organization who didn't understand what friendship was or how honorable Sam

Caliban was. And one other thing though it probably wasn't necessary to mention it. Mr Ziff would do everything he could and would take the heat off, but he did have this responsibility to the stockholders. It was an awkward thing, but he did have this responsibility.

Mr Caliban got the picture. He went into action right away. But he didn't want to dig into his capital, not yet anyway. Hell, he could always take up a few rugs, and there were the paintings, but those were his insurance. They would see to it that Jerry could go to Harvard no matter what. The idea was to send Jerry to Harvard and then to the Harvard Law School so he could come out knowing enough to take care of problems just like this and save the family thousands in legal fees. Mr Caliban had one more card to play before he dug into his capital. He would bankroll Nick the Greek. There was no better man with the dice anywhere and he made his living out of situations just like this. Nick the Greek always gambled on other people's money and then took a cut of the winnings, a healthy cut, but Nick the Greek was worth it. He had no money of his own, he lived too high, but there was no better man with the dice. And Nick the Greek was a friend from way back. There was the time when Nick had had a heart attack. He had just crumpled over with the dice in his fist. At the admissions desk a nurse bent down over the stretcher and asked Nick the Greek for his health insurance card. He didn't have one. The nurse asked to see a bank statement. Nick muttered, he was in great pain, that he wasn't in the habit of carrying his fucking bank statement around with him. It was three in the morning, so they couldn't telephone the bank, and Nick didn't have a bank account then anyway. All he had was the money he had been bankrolled with and that couldn't be used for a heart attack. The nurse was sorry, but they could not admit anyone without proof that he could pay the bill. The hospital would go broke letting just any sick person in. Nick told the nurse to get in touch with Sam Caliban. Nick almost died, but

Mr Caliban took care of things, and Nick had been in his debt ever since, morally. Nick would be only too happy to win back Mr Caliban's money. You needed a friend in this world. It was a tough world, but if you knew the right people it made things a little easier.

Jerry and I went to Palm Springs the day Nick the Greek was to start winning back Mr Caliban's money. It was Easter vacation. I felt bad that I was going to miss Easter Sunday mass with my father, but the Palm Springs prospects looked too good. Mr Caliban had lent his new girl friend to Jerry, because Mr and Mrs Caliban went to Hawaii every Easter, it was a family tradition. Tanya was every bit as sensational as Jerry had described. It was too bad she couldn't act, she had star quality.

We were driving through Banning in the yellow Mercury. I was sitting in the back and when I leaned forward to look at the speedometer I could smell Tanya's perfume. Jerry was doing ninety.

'Hit a hundred Jerry, and I'll come,' Tanya said, 'I swear I will.' He did. Tanya moved her bottom around and I craned to get a look. Her dress slid up her legs. 'I came, I swear I did. God, you're a great driver.' She put her head in Jerry's lap and made cheetah noises. Now I couldn't see anything but I could tell what she was up to.

In about two miles Jerry cried 'Shee-it!' and Tanya asked for his handkerchief. He didn't have one, so I handed mine over. I told her to keep it. The Joshua trees were there, Mt San Jacinto had snow on it. A cop stopped us.

'You were doing a hundred and five, buddy.'

Jerry handed the cop a card. The cop said okay, but keep to the speed limit. Tanya said Mr Caliban had given her one of the cards too.

It was pleasant sitting by the pool watching Tanya dive in with hardly a ripple, but at night she and Jerry had each other and I had only *The Autobiography of Lincoln Steffens*. I read about how Steffens had had his first ejaculation back in the nineteenth century exercising horses around Sacramento, but through the wall noises of love disturbed my concentration. Tanya had tremendous energy and a wide vocabulary in her field. I came to admire her during those few days. I knew she had been petulant and difficult with Mr Caliban but with Jerry she was just plain fun. She seemed at peace with herself and displayed a unity of mind and body that would confound philosophers. Jerry spoke to me privately of marrying her after he finished law school. His father would be well into his sixties by then and might not mind giving her up. Gratifying as a friend's happiness can be, I wanted more for myself. My chief purpose in coming to Palm Springs had been to find Linda and to probe her interest in me. We had conversed in class, but all I really knew about her was that she shared my enthusiasm for Willa Cather's descriptions of sod houses in Nebraska. The rest was rumor. I made a tour of the motels and discovered her alone by a pool unscrewing the cap on a bottle of Sea and Ski.

'Let me do that for you,' I said, very bold.

She acquiesced. Imagine my delight. I could touch her everywhere her bathing suit was not, and all for a perfectly legitimate purpose, to shield her flesh from harsh rays. She was like Lauren Bacall only a little less angular. The cream spread easily. I spread it gently, firmly, gently, lingering over her slim feet, which I had never before seen out of shoes, and when I ventured near the bottom of her suit, she didn't stop me on either side. I bought us cokes and we discussed who else was in P.S.

'I came down with Sharon. She's been seeing this guy.'

'You seeing anyone?'

'Sure. I don't know how I feel about Marty any more. You know Marty? He goes to U.C.L.A.'

'Is he the big guy I've seen you with? He must be a jock.'

'Football. All he cares about is football. 'Course he's in love with me.'

'You in love with him?'

75

'I don't think I'm in love with anybody right now. We're lavaliered though. I think I want somebody more intellectual.'

'Listen. We could go to a movie tonight.'

We went to see Fred Astaire and Leslie Caron in *Daddy Long Legs*. Linda leaned over and told me that she had gone to a movie with a guy once who had made a hole in the bottom of the popcorn box and put himself through it, and when she grabbed for popcorn she screamed and slapped him. After that we giggled every time we ate the popcorn, and we held hands for about the last fifteen minutes of the movie. I had borrowed Jerry's car. I didn't have a license but he had given me the card. I drove out into the desert, asking Linda questions so I could listen to her voice. I liked her voice so much that I had telephoned her often just to hear her say hello. Then I would hang up. She didn't know this, of course, and I was smart enough not to tell her. Now I felt I could listen to her voice forever as we drove in the dark. I told her how much I admired her essays in English class and she said they weren't as good as mine. I told her she had wit and sophistication and that she didn't walk like the other girls. She walked like a model or a person with dignity. She asked didn't I know that a lot of people hated her.

'Some people say you're a bitch,' I said. 'I don't think so. I think those people are inferior.'

'I hate them,' she said. 'I hate them so much I'd like to see them die. Don't you hate some people that way?'

'I don't think I hate anybody. I'm not sure.'

'That's remarkable,' Linda said.

I pulled off the road and parked in the desert. I started to say something but Linda told me to kiss her. We played with each other's tongues and pressed our teeth together.

'That's the first time I ever kissed a Catholic,' Linda said.

'Was it nice?'

'Yes.'

We kissed some more. I tried to put my hands in places but

she did things with her arms and hands to keep me off, so I concentrated on the kissing.

'I have to get back,' she said, and she drew away.

'Why?'

'I'm sorry. I promised I'd meet Marty. You know. We are lavaliered.'

'But you said you didn't love him.'

'I know. But I have to get back. He'll be mad.' She laughed a little. I said I guessed it was pretty funny, she and I like this, with them lavaliered and Marty waiting. We talked about love and marriage on the way back. She wanted to stay free all her life, whether she was married or not. Her mother got after her all the time. Her mother acted as though there were no such things as contraceptives. Linda said she was going to take a trip to Europe that summer and her mother wouldn't be able to know what she was up to and neither would Marty. When I let her off I opened the door for her and kissed her right there in the street. Linda said she liked that and I was very brave because Marty was probably watching out the window of her motel room. She wanted to see me again. She'd let me know.

When I got back to our motel I had some gin and orange juice with Tanya and Jerry in their room. Tanya was wearing a black diaphanous nightie that disturbed me. I had stone ache.

'Well,' Jerry said, 'whad'ja catch?'

'We made out,' I said. 'Nothing much.'

'I'll bet,' Jerry said, and Tanya rolled over on him.

I dreamt that Linda was waiting for me at the head of a long, broad winding staircase. Wind billowed curtains at high windows and stringed instruments played. We made love until I was lifted out of her arms by a whirlwind. I landed on a beach. The sun was hot and I looked out at a rock in the water. Linda was impaled, naked lying on her back, on the point of the rock. Blood poured out of her, washing away in the waves. What a beautiful dream, I thought. This must be love.

ELEVEN

Encore Brentwood

At the Calibans one of the Picassos and the Rouault Christ were gone. Nick the Greek had fucked up. Mrs Caliban had believed that the threat had been against another Sam Caliban, but now she had to face facts. Her horse racing allowance was cut in half.

'How do you expect me to live?' she said. 'I suppose I'll be back scrubbing floors again.'

'Relax, Bear,' Mr Caliban said. 'I wouldn't let Irma go for anything.'

'You care more about Irma than you do about me.'

'You are number one in my life,' Mr Caliban said. 'Why don't you go to the track every other day? That way you won't notice the difference.'

'It's not the same,' she said. 'It's just not the same. Oh, Sammy. What are we going to do?'

'I'm going to make five pictures this year instead of three, that's what we're going to do. Ain't no tragedy.'

'You'll kill yourself. You've got to take care of yourself. Why don't we join a health club? I could lose a few pounds.'

'I like you just the way you are, Little Bear.'

'I'm a nervous wreck. I can't sleep since this. If I take any more pills I'll be a psychotic. Dr Orloff said so.'

'You still seeing him?'

'You know he's the only one I ever liked. He's the only one who ever listens, really listens to me. You're too busy to listen to me.'

'Pay me fifty bucks an hour and I'd listen to anything.'

'You're being cruel.'

'I didn't mean it.'

'You're being cruel to your Bear. You've never been cruel to your Bear before. My God what's happening to you? The world comes crashing down on me and what do I get from you but cruel? The El Dorado doesn't run right, you've known it for weeks and you don't do anything about it. You don't care if I get killed on the freeway. I think you want me to get killed. I don't care about the plot against you. What about the plot against me?'

'Look,' Mr Caliban said, 'I'll take the El Dorado, you take the De Ville. How's that?'

'Better.'

But her anxieties were too deep-seated to be assuaged by comforting gestures. It was easier to be poor than to be rich and to feel poised over a financial abyss. Her judgment of horse flesh was affected. It looked as though her allowance wouldn't last the Hollywood Park meeting, and by opening day at Santa Anita she might be destitute. One night in frustration she ripped the stuffing out of Big Bear. Mr Caliban came into Jerry's room.

'It's going to cost me a good two hundred to get that animal restuffed,' he said with a trace of bitterness.

'Throw it out,' Jerry suggested.

'I couldn't do that,' Mr Caliban said. 'You know what those animals mean to your mother. She didn't mean to do it. She doesn't know what she's doing. I think she needs round the clock care.'

'Have her committed,' Jerry said.

'I couldn't do that,' Mr Caliban said. 'Maybe some guys would do that, but I couldn't. We came up together. We went through everything together. Sometimes one partner grows and the other doesn't. I'm not the same person I was. She probably never should of given up her career. But she wanted to be home with the kids. It's hard on a woman. I was thinking I'd get a nurse to live in.'

'That would cost you,' Jerry said.

'So I'm Sam Caliban I have to worry about every dollar? I'm going to let my wife suffer because I'm too cheap? I guess they don't teach you no ethics.'

'I'm sorry,' Jerry said.

'This is hard on everybody.'

'At least you have Tanya.'

'That cunt,' Mr Caliban said. 'I think I picked up a dose from her.'

'Jesus,' Jerry said.

'You better get yourself checked,' Mr Caliban said.

Mrs Caliban went downhill. She was picked up selling grapefruit without a permit on the corner of Roxbury and little Santa Monica. The papers never got hold of it, but strings had to be pulled. I tried to talk to her.

'You've got to calm down, Mrs Caliban. You've been like a mother to me. You don't know how grateful I am. You're a wonderful person. Why punish yourself?'

'Stop burning my face. You're burning my face.'

'I'm trying to help you. I care for you. We all care for you.'

'You don't know the half of it.' She was lying in her chartreuse, bears about, glum. 'All my life. You don't know. You would never guess, would you. Stop doing that with your hands. I have washed toilets. You wash a toilet, you feel like a toilet. Him with his nose in the air. He's got me dancing on a string, break it, and he don't care. He thinks he made me. Well what is he now, a fat little nothing. I had an affair with Bruce Cabot. I can still belt them out.' She sang.

They put her on a new pill. It made her happy as a child. Mr Caliban bought her toy horses for her birthday. She arranged them about her bed and gave them names, Wuzza-Wuzza, Bonwit, Michigan Avenue, Smacky Lips, Wan Q, Frank, Cry Tomorrow.

My work was suffering. I did a lot of staring, I fell down in Latin and gave a rotten performance at the Roman banquet, ill at ease in my toga, stumbling through a speech that depended on a perfect execution of the fifth declension, at a loss for endings. I missed a bunt on a squeeze play and just stood there in the box as the runner was tagged out and crashed into me. I didn't like to admit it, but I had allowed myself to become dependent on the stability of the Calibans, and as they fell apart I was falling with them. The nurse guarded Mrs Caliban, and Mr Caliban and Jerry were hardly ever home. Mr Caliban would go to see Tanya after he finished shooting every day, and Jerry would slip it to her on the sly after his father left. They were both on penicillin. I was in a fever fit over Linda, but I was unable to get her to do more than have lunch with me a couple of times a week. We would sit on the great lawn of the high school looking over the tree choked streets of Beverly Hills, discussing literature and her campaign for student body secretary. I was to make her nomination speech and had been boning up on Calhoun. She feared her tits would lose her votes with the girls, I said damn the petty resentments of underlings. She couldn't go out with me, she said, Marty was too cross. He had confessed Linda's infidelity to his fraternity brothers, and they had made things worse by razzing him at a stag party, comparing a woman and a donkey in a pornographic movie to Linda and me. I cherished my minutes with her but I was dying for it. When she talked I looked into her mouth. At home I searched the TV Guide for Lauren Bacall movies. At mass I tried to steady myself, but I was beginning to lose my faith.

Then Granny died, just dropped her face into a plate of stew one night and died. My father wanted to bury her at sea but could not figure out how, and he was unsure what to do with a Methodist corpse. When I arrived Granny was stretched on the dining room table. Old Glory covered her.

'We had a burial at sea in the Aleutians,' Dad said. 'That Jap

81

officer I captured jumped overboard. They're a proud people, the Japanese. He froze to death in thirty seconds. We gave him the full rites though. He was a very educated man, spoke fifteen languages. I'd like to do the same for your mother's mother. She was a good old dame, son.'

He pulled back the flag before I could turn away.

'She had terrific spirit,' Dad said. 'Her morale was tops, right to the end. She fought right to the bell.'

But we determined that burial at sea in port was impractical. We let Forest Lawn cook her. My father said she had left no will and she had no money. When I had been about five years old I had asked her if she would marry me when I grew up. She had said that I would probably find somebody else, but she promised me her engagement ring for my bride. It was a big diamond and I wondered where it had gone. Her hands were bare. My father said she had probably sold it, years before. I helped him fill out an interment arrangements form. Disposition: cremation. Casket: $265.00. Outside case: none. Embalming or preparing: no. Hearse: none. Limousines: none. Flower car: none. Clothing: no. Disposition of Jewelry: no. Cemetery charges: self. Newspaper: no. Floral crepe or flowers: no. Music—Soloist—Organist—: no. Eligibility for burial benefits: So. Sec. 567-18-9302. Filing fee: $5.00. Tax: @ 2% $5.30. Total: $275.30. They had a minister there who could handle anything.

'Bereft are her children, but she lives in memory . . .' My father and I were the only mourners. I wrote a letter to Mother and got an answer weeks later saying good riddance.

Dad was pretty lonely. He took to telephoning me during the week and at breakfast after mass he would ask me to think about moving in with him because a father and a son ought to be together. We could have good times. Life was short. I thought it over. Caliban days weren't what they had been. Linda wouldn't have me. Dad needed me. I could help him out. Being much indisposed in both mind and body, incapable of diverting myself either with company or books, and yet in a condition that made some diversion necessary, I was glad of anything that would engage my attention, without fatiguing it. I would go home. On my last night at the Calibans I had another pleasant dream. I was sitting on Josef Stalin's knee, confiding to him in fluent Russian the kindness and good will of the American people. He seemed impressed.

TWELVE

The Old Hollywood

For a man devoted to naval standards, my father had allowed his house to degenerate in matters of hygiene. So low in his mind had he become, and so demoralized was his command by Granny's surly conduct, that when he had run out of things to do for the Church, he would lie abed, hour after hour, leaving undone the simple tasks that distinguish man from brute, the farmer from his animals. On watch one night, I heard with a start a distant rending crash coming from his bedroom off the galley. I hurried down to find him breathless and entangled in the wreckage of his bed. It seems that the wire mattress, rusted and rotted by his nocturnal diuresis, a condition attributable wholly to his state of mind, which caused him to forget to do things the rest of us accomplish through habit and instinct, had collapsed under his weight.

'What happened?' I asked.

'Can't you see, Salty?' he said, for Salty is what he had taken to calling me. 'The whole shooting gallery collapsed under me.'

Immediately commencing carpenter, I built him a special platform to sleep on, so contrived that his wastes would pass through the bottom of it; an enameled pan placed under him received whatsoever fell, which being duly emptied and washed, he was thus kept perfectly sweet and clean. Towards my labors he assumed a more benevolent than a grateful attitude, for it was the key to the relations we established, that he was helping me, not I him. As I sawed and joined, he would interject 'That's right,' 'Just so,' 'A little more to the left,' 'You're getting it now,' 'Watch that bulkhead,' 'I was afraid that would happen,' 'You're forcing it, it's like a horse, you've got to give him his head,' and like exhortations, though the construction was my own contrivance, and had I offered him the tools of a professional carpenter, a diagram simple enough for a child, and a hundred dollar bet, a straitjacketed lunatic would have had a better chance of building the bed than he. Still, when he was not giving advice, he entertained me with a narrative of changing naval bunk design, from the days of the hammock onward, with digressions concerning where to stow your duffle bag and how he dealt with cases of veneral disease under his command.

I had a great deal of construction work and general tidying up to do during those first weeks, and he always took the same benevolent attitude toward my efforts, as though he was glad to see I was not idle or degenerate, like the rest of modern youth. I suppose he suspected the worst of my life with the Calibans. I was pleased to see that my busyness buoyed him a little. He began to spend less time in bed. He felt himself responsible that I did things properly and that I was kept occupied.

When I had disinfected the galley, ridding it of mold, roaches, and miscellaneous garbage, he had me take inventory of its salvaged contents: a mixed set of crockery for two, three forks, two spoons, one knife, coffee pot, pot, roasting pan, one gas mask functioning, one gas mask non-functioning, one bottle ketchup half full, one bottle ketchup one quarter full, framed glassed photograph of Captain in beachmaster's garb blowing whistle, one stove (oven door hingeless from explosion caused by Chief Petty Officer's negligence), one chair assigned oven door holding shut detail, one O-So-Cool. This last was a self-sustaining cooling box, invented by the British army for action on the Indian sub-continent. You poured water over porous sides and top to activate natural evaporative cooling process. The O-So-Cool cut refrigeration cost factor at equipment purchase and energy unit per month billing levels.

Galley inventory, repeated weekly, proved so successful that I was assigned to take inventory of the other rooms as well.

'I've never really known what I've had, Salty,' Dad said, 'and if a man don't know what he has, he's in trouble, because how's he going to know if somebody comes along and takes it away from him?'

I agreed with the principle, and I was glad to see him enter into inventory spirit, hovering near me, making sure I caught every last item. His day room offered the greatest riches. It was a museum and library of his life. It had to be set in order, if that life was to go forward.

We began with his address and telephone book, thick with hundreds of entries.

'I didn't used to need that,' Dad said. 'My secretaries used to do all my contacting for me. But you have to adjust.'

I suggested that we proceed in two stages. Since the earliest entries dated from the 1920s, it was safe to assume that many of these were now inaccurate, that people had moved, changed telephone numbers, or died. He would know of most of the deaths, as he had attended most of the funerals. We would eliminate the deceased first; then we would go on to check the accuracy of surviving entries and make a fresh, new list that would enable him to reach people with maximum speed and accuracy. It would be a hell of a big operation, but if we pushed ahead and cut down on the coffee breaks, we could beat this thing and come in ahead of schedule. That would put us ahead of the game.

As I would call out a name, however, he would want to know whether I knew the person.

'Sy Lesser,' I would say, pencil at the ready, and he:

'Sy Lesser. Do you remember him, Salty?'

'I think he was before my time.'

'Sy Lesser. He was quite a character. He used to come up to the ranch with Big Boy Williams. Big Boy was hitting the bottle pretty hard in those days. I remember his wife. But Sy, he gave me the best deal anyone ever had on a picture up to that time. I got a cut of the profits. That paid for plenty of dresses for your Ma, not that I minded it, not a bit, the mother of my son. She was a great gal, Salty, in those days, and I don't know whatever got into her to break up the family. I'll tell you about it someday, when you're old enough to understand.

'Frankly, Sy was a little fella, and when he'd come up to the ranch with Big Boy, we used to put Sy on horseback, we put him on old Charlie, I think it was, and Sy was scared to death, and Padre Maguire was up at the ranch one time, when Sy was there with Big Boy Williams. You remember Padre Maguire. He wrote 'Praise the Lord and Pass the Ammunition.' A real character.

> Praise the Lord and pass the ammunition,
> Praise the Lord and pass the ammunition,
> Praise the Lord and pass the ammunition,
> And we'll all go free.

He'll be in the book there, we'll come to him when we get to the M's. They're next, aren't they? M comes after L, that's right.

'Anyhow, Sy was up at the ranch with Big Boy and Padre Maguire, and Sy was on old Charlie. Now old Charlie was so old, the boys used to say the stable could of burned down around his ears and he'd never notice. I don't know what got into old Charlie that time, but he took off down the hill towards the old beach house with Sy hanging on for dear life, hollering at the top of his lungs, see.

'No, I'd been in a lot of pictures, and I'd always done all my own stunts, you remember that, and when I saw old Charlie take off with Sy down the hill, I looked around for Tom. Tom died during the war, it nearly broke my heart. I gave a whistle,

Phweet!, and Tom come running, just like he always did, and I got a running start and jumped aboard old Tom right up over his hind-quarters—there's a trick to it, you give yourself a little boost with the hands right under the crotch, here—bareback, with no saddle, there wasn't time to saddle up. And I lit out after Sy.

'Tom was plenty fast, and a lot faster than old Charlie, and Tom and I caught up to Sy and old Charlie in about two, maybe three hundred yards. I drew along side, we must of been doing thirty-forty mile an hour, and I just reached over and pulled Sy right out of the saddle and set him down right in front of me on Tom. I'd done a scene like that in .45 *Caliber*, I think it was, or *Arizona Justice*, only then I grabbed Frank Kohler off a locomotive. Well, be that as it may, let me tell you Salty, when we got back to the house old Sy was white as a sheet. And you know what Padre Maguire did then? This is the clincher, right here.

'To make a long story short, Padre Maguire gave old Sy the last rites! Can you top that? The last rites! The Padre was a great one for the ribbing. Sy wasn't even a Catholic, you know, he was a Jewish fella. But a wonderful guy, and a great sport. He died in 1936. May of '36. I went to the funeral. We weren't supposed to go in those days, or some people said. But I was always ahead of the times. You got to be. I remember his widow. She was pretty broke up about it. Women take these things hard. The way I figure, when your number's up. Sy died of a heart attack in the middle of a picture we were making out at Newhall. She never married again. She was a loyal gal, Salty.'

Since each of the entries called forth biography, sorting out the book occupied many weeks; and while I have ever loved scholarship, my ardor sometimes flagged. My father, however, thrived on the work, and such impatience as I felt was balanced by the pleasure I took in seeing him so happily engaged. When I would reach a point of absolute stultification, unable to grasp the pencil longer, the names blurs, my brain dissolving with Hollywood, I would go into the bathroom and think about Linda. The memory of our desert rendezvous cheered me and cleared my head. Once more I would be spreading the cream over her long body, to and fro, fro to. At that moment Jerry was probably giving it to Tanya from behind or getting his cock sucked. Refreshed, I returned to the work. By the time we reached the O's, it had become apparent that most of these persons were dead, and for a time I feared Dad might suffer a depression, counting so many of his friends among the fallen. But the opposite was true, for as the corpses piled up, until I began to feel familiar with the occupants of a large percentage of all the graves in Southern California, and death seemed palpable about me, he brightened with every case, and his anecdotes became more vivid, humorous, and rich with detail. He was impressed not so much that hundreds had vanished from this world as that he was still living in it. He spoke of fooling the insurance companies and of the rewards of sensible diet and vigorous physical exercise. With each of the departed, he took note of the cause of death and delivered himself of an opinion how the life might have been extended, the day of expiration postponed. Eddie Dwyer had died of an enlarged liver but he, my father, had always gone easy on the booze and now took none. Nat Liebeskind had died of lung cancer, but my father confined himself to an after dinner cigar and did not inhale. F. W. Murnau had been killed in a motoring accident, but my father always drove cautiously and had lightning reflexes. You could spot signs of decay, as in Sol Howard, who had gone bald at thirty, but my father always dried his head thoroughly after a shower. The anus was an important thing. My father always washed it thoroughly with soap and warm water after defecating, unless he was caught in a public place, and the upshot of it was, he had the anus of a man half his age. If I wasn't taking care of myself down there, I had better hop to it.

89

As it happened, three names survived our pruning of the dead, Marshall Marshall, John Ford, and my mother. I entered her Roman address. Marshall Marshall was an automobile salesman who had interested my father in the John Birch Society. Marshall had been divorced by Colonel Jacob Ruppert's granddaughter and had got himself baptized a Catholic in consequence. My father told me that it was Marshall's discovery that a recent failure of the cranberry crop was a communist plot to undermine the integrity of the Thanksgiving dinner. This seemed to me doubtful, but my father said that he always respected another man's beliefs. The addresses and telephone numbers for Marshall and Ford proved accurate. How would I like to meet Marshall Marshall? I replied that I would be delighted to meet him and that I had an interest equally lively in meeting John Ford, whom I took to be the greatest genius in the history of the American cinema and whose *The Long Voyage Home*, which I had seen at the age of eight, had affected me so deeply, that I had wept over it.

'There's nothing wrong with a man crying,' said my father, and tears formed in his eyes and dripped down his face. I didn't know what I had said.

I asked him what was the trouble, and he said that he had been thinking about what a foolish thing it had been for 'your Ma' to break up the family; he had offered her anything she had wanted; he had given her a separate bedroom, he had had the idea that they could open a dude ranch together and invite old friends from the pioneer days of Hollywood up to tell stories, sing songs, and entertain the guests generally. People from Omaha didn't know what they were missing. Or he and Mother could have done an Osa and Martin Johnson thing, bring back films of bushmen or some of the Peruvian or Bolivian Indians who were on dope all the time and syndicate it for television. It was his ambition to have a ranch again some day, with a place to hang up his spurs. There wasn't room here, he couldn't unpack. His old black saddle with the silver trimmings was out in the garage under newspapers, maybe I had noticed it. We could drop in on Marshall at the Chevrolet agency.

THIRTEEN

Santa Monica

We encountered Marshall Marshall at a propitious moment on the floor of the display salon, just as he was completing the sale of a Bel-Air. As was his practice, he offered as a bonus to the automobile contract a free copy of the collected speeches of Robert Welch, founder of the John Birch Society, and a year's free subscription to *American Opinion*, organ of the Society. In this instance the customer refused the bonus, shoving the speeches aside and threatening to back out of the deal.

'I came here to buy a Chevrolet,' he said, 'not a crack-pot philosophy.'

I admired the good humor with which Marshall accepted the rebuff. He was like the street evangelist who endures cheerfully the boorish ignorance of the unsaved. Marshall was a big, tall fellow, overweight, with the face of a middle-aged cherub and the proud bearing of a former Marine Corps officer. We repaired with him to a coffee shop. He and my father ordered apple pie and coffee, I elected cherry pie and a glass of milk.

Marshall asked me about my studies, his voice soft yet manly, with the pleasant slow vowels and muffled consonants of his native North Carolina. He was especially interested in how American history was being taught at my high school. He had been a history teacher himself, before he had got into the automobile business, and he was still a historian and always would be. Were they emphasizing that America was a Republic, not a democracy? I said I was uncertain of the distinction, and he explained it to me, forcefully, logically, and with impressive citations from the Constitution and the Federalist Papers. He praised Senator McCarthy, comparing him to Patrick Henry, John Calhoun, Henry Clay, Robert E. Lee, Attorney General Palmer, and St Stephen, the first martyr, who, Marshall had just learned from a book loaned him by his parish priest, had been stoned to death for his beliefs. When I asked Marshall whether he thought that Senator McCarthy's methods were sometimes excessive, he cautioned me, his big round face radiating benignity and faith, that the cost of liberty was always high. I did not mention that I had written Edward R. Murrow a fan letter complimenting him on his McCarthy broadcasts, expressing my hope that Murrow would succeed in driving that alcoholic perverted psychopath to an early grave. Marshall was too sincere for argument.

He was pleased with the sale of the Bel-Air. It would mean at least thirty dollars to him, and it placed him two cars ahead of his nearest competitor at the agency for salesman of the month. When my father abandoned us for a moment, saying he had to go pump the bilge, Marshall leaned forward and said to me in confidential tones, that my father was the greatest man he had ever met, and that it was his ambition, once he had built up sufficient savings from Chevrolet sales, to produce a motion picture version of the life of General MacArthur, with my father as the star. It would get my father's career rolling again, he said, and stand as a lasting tribute to two great Americans.

'Do you have a lot of contacts in the industry, Mr Marshall?' I asked.

'You don't need contacts for a thing like this,' Marshall said. 'What you need is dedication. I know some people at Armed Forces Radio, they are very fired up about this project. I call it Project Return. If you break the code, you see it gets in what General MacArthur said about returning to the Philippines and your father's return to the screen. It can't miss.'

'I have some industry contacts myself,' I said. 'I know a man who never lost money on a picture.'

'That's quite a record,' Marshall said. 'Who is he?'

'I don't know that I should give out his name, but he told me some of his secrets. I'd be happy to pass them on to someone like yourself.'

'Let's get right on this,' Marshall said. 'I learned in the Marine Corps that procrastination is the thief of time. You and your Dad come over to my place tonight. I'll fix supper and we'll have a background and general strategy planning session.'

When my father returned, we set the meeting back a week because Dad said he had a lot of paperwork and it would take him several days of going at it head to head before he could get out from under. My father paid the check with a hundred-dollar bill and pressed a dollar tip directly into the waitress's hand:

'This is for you, dear. That's some apple pie.'

Marshall had sold my father the DeSoto and they had got into the habit of shooting the breeze when the DeSoto needed an oil change. When DeSotos became extinct, Marshall had switched to Chevrolets. There was less prestige but steadier sales. The transition had been rough on him because his wife had dumped him at the time, and he had to adjust to bachelorhood and Chevrolets all at once. She was one of those flighty women, my father said. Kind of a socialite. Well old Marsh hadn't been social enough for her. There had been a kid. He lived with his mother now but Marsh was saving up to send him to Notre Dame one day. Marsh had taken the divorce pretty hard, but then he got very sincere about politics and he found the Church. A convert can have a strong faith. They were all converts in the old days, Jesus Himself was a convert, you could say. Marsh sort of looked up to my father as a father, and my father was glad to pass on to him some of the lessons life had taught, such as how to keep punching. Marsh had his head above water now and he had a great future if he would keep an even keel. He was working out a deal for my father for a new Chevrolet without ash trays, sun visors, arm rests, or plush carpeting that nobody needed. You had to order special from the factory and it paid to know somebody. He helped Marsh out with advice and Marsh helped him. The politicians called it log rolling.

We started brainstorming after the meatloaf. Marshall had a big coffee pot so we could keep at it all night if we had to. He showed us the story treatment he had worked up:

> General of the Army Douglas MacArthur was the greatest patriot this Republic has known since the late and great General Robert E. Lee. We see him smashing the Red Bonus Marchers. We see him rescuing our Filipino brethren. We see him teaching the broken back Japanese how to govern themselves without falling prey to the Red Russians and the Red Chinese. We see him on the brink of saving the free world in Korea only to be done in by comsymp politicians whose names every patriot knows by heart. We see him mobbed by throngs in San Francisco. We see him addressing the weak-kneed Congress of the U.S. Dissolve to copy of U.S. Constitution. A woolly head sets fire to the document and burns it up.

I told Marshall that the story was impressive but that as a property it lacked the common touch. My industry contacts told me that the key to movie success was having your hand on the pulse of the people. I could see that it would be easier to do a picture on Harry Truman because everyone knew he washed his own underwear. People could identify with that.

'Truman was a Red,' Marshall said.

'That may be,' I said, 'but he washed his underwear and he went for walks. And there was the story about him and Bess breaking the bed in the White House. People could identify with that, see what I mean?'

'General MacArthur never did anything like that,' Marshall said.

'Then we've got problems,' I said. 'He must have done something. Didn't he drink or gamble or fool around with women?'

'Certainly not.'

'Well something. You've got to have that common touch. Even the old Greeks knew that. *Oedipus* wouldn't have them standing in line for thousands of years if the hero didn't actually sleep with his mother. Look at Hamlet, he's no angel. Or nearer home take *Gone With the Wind.*'

'Greatest picture of all time,' Marshall said.

'Right. But look at Scarlett and Rhett. Naughty, right?'

'You've got a point,' Marshall said.

'Now who is the greatest hero of all time?'

'Jesus Christ.'

'All right,' I said, 'I'll tell you something. If I was making a picture about Jesus Christ, I'd play up the anger in the temple thing, the fainthearted thing in the Garden of Gethsemane. And I'd get a knockout to play Mary Magdalene. You see it? The human element. Now can't you think of any little flaw in General MacArthur?'

Marshall thought. He paced up and down. He started to sweat. Looking for flaws in General MacArthur was very painful for him. He couldn't think of any. At last my father, who hadn't been in the business for nothing, remembered that MacArthur's uniform was often untidy. His cap was frayed, he rarely wore a tie, and he looked pretty wrinkled.

'That wasn't a flaw,' Marshall said. 'That was his mystique.'

'We'll make it both,' I said. 'It's just what we need. We'll show him having an argument with his wife "Douglas, that uniform is a disgrace. Go out and buy yourself a new one." "Woman, I have no time for shopping. Manila has fallen." '

'The kid's got imagination, Marsh,' my father said.

'Maybe you're right,' Marshall said. 'I'm coming around to you fellows' point of view. It's just that with such a great man,

I wouldn't want to do anything to tarnish the image. I've taken an oath on that. It's a question of honor with me.'

'There isn't enough honor left in the world,' my father said. 'It's guys like you who keep this country great.'

'Coming from you, Captain,' Marshall said, 'that's quite a compliment. You know you're the only man I'd let play the General.'

'Why don't we sleep on it?' my father said. 'No sense rushing into things. We could make these sessions a regular thing. Keep us on our toes.'

Marshall was thrilled with the idea. But he hoped we wouldn't go yet. He had received an abusive letter from his ex-wife that he needed my father's advice on. My father was the only man he knew who could handle women. The letter questioned whether Marshall should be taken seriously as a human being. It said that in reality he was a baby, a totally irresponsible, selfish, self-seeking, self-deluded, pompous, puffed-up and empty baby. As things were, he did little to inspire respect. If he thought she was accepting any shit shavings he happened to have left over from his larger pile, he was mistaken. He would have to come to terms with reality.

'That kind of thing hurts,' my father said, 'even when we know it's just a dame blowing off steam. Don't let it get you down. We've all been through it. I'll have one more cuppa Joe before we shove off.'

'I feel better just talking to you, Captain.'

'You behind in the old alimony again?'

He was. He didn't know where the money went. My father told him to keep track of everything and save all his receipts.

In the DeSoto I told my father that Marshall seemed very fond of him.

'He's a lonely fellow,' my father said. 'I noticed his weight going up. He needs to get out into the fresh air.'

'Do you think this picture will come to anything?'

'You never can tell. He needs capital. The banks control

everything these days. Some Wall Street lawyer. They tell us what to do and they never cleaned a stable. You can't tell about these things. I never give up on anything. I liked what you said in there tonight. You got horse sense. You could walk into a board room right now and tell them where to get off. Between the two of us, son, you've got it up here and I've got the experience that nothing else can teach you, we could go places. Of course, poor old Marsh, he ain't going nowhere, you know what I mean?'

FOURTEEN

Bel-Air

We approached John Ford in the church parking lot after twelve o'clock mass, as he was being assisted into a black Thunderbird by his driver. Ford had often directed my father but, so my mother told me, had snubbed Dad for many years after an unfortunate incident in Shanghai, the particulars of which I never learned, except that my father was supposed to have abandoned Ford when the latter was in a condition requiring assistance. Preparatory to the encounter, my father had briefed me extensively, speaking of the great man with affection and respect, though it was Dad's opinion that Ford ought never to have made *The Grapes of Wrath*: in so doing Ford had made himself, however innocently, a purveyor of communist-socialist propaganda. I offered that the film was nevertheless intensely moving and a piece of high cinematic art. My father said that this was just the trouble.

I had rehearsed a speech, intending to deliver it at the earliest possible opportunity, to convey my admiration. But when my father greeted Ford as 'old shipmate' and introduced me first as his uncle and then as his 'son Salty, my manager, and a helluva first baseman, Jack, and a pretty fair dishwasher too,' I was made awkward by these encomiums and was able to express only the most conventional of greetings.

Ford invited us up to his house for breakfast. As we followed the Thunderbird along Sunset into Bel-Air, my father showed signs of unease, saying that we could not stay long, that he

would probably just have coffee, that he had some bills to pay
and paperwork, that Ford was a busy man and we must not
his abuse hospitality, but Ford would be of great help to me in
my career and that I should show my stuff. What he meant by
this advice I do not know, for as yet I had no career, nor had I
the least intention of involving myself in the movies or anything remotely connected to showbiz. No child aspires to re-
peat the tragedy of his parents but must avert the compulsion
to do so.

The house was grand in the Spanish style, with a swimming
pool and a tennis court, and it was strange to see my father
there. His own house was by comparison a shack, yet I knew
that Casa Fiesta had been more splendorous than this and that
then my father could have invited Ford, now he could not. We
sat in a great room by a fragrant eucalyptus fire, Ford and his
wife, Mary, and I sipping bloody marys, my father tomato
juice; then a fine big breakfast and afterwards coffee with Irish
whiskey in it. I was grateful to Ford for pressing drink on me.
I had begun to think my drinking days were over and had even
thought of Anatol with a certain wistfulness. Of course my
father disapproved, though quietly, for he said I had to make
up my own mind about such things and here he seemed to wish
to defer to Ford.

'You didn't make Admiral for nothing, Jack,' my father
said.

Around us were displayed the symbols and tokens of Ford's
achievements, the Academy Award Oscars, film festival prizes,
medals from this and that, honors bestowed by kings, queens,
taoiseachs and presidents. My father was very quiet and glanced
often at his watch, a weighty piece with several dials which had
been presented to him by a frogman. Ford was frail in body
but lively in intellect. My father had briefed me that Ford was
disinclined to wear underwear, and in fact never wore it,
except under arctic conditions, and while I could not verify
this, I noted that he was dressed in other ways casually, in

100

loose-fitting trousers and safari shirt, with an ascot at the throat. Of his eyes I could detect very little. One looked out from behind a thick, dark lens, the other was covered by a black patch.

When Ford was well into his coffee, he made some effort to take an interest in me, asking what was my favorite subject in school, and when I said English, he inquired which were my favorite English authors. I said Swift. Ford protested that Swift was not English but Irish, though a Protestant, and asked did I know the *Drapier's Letters*. I did not, so he gave me a concise account of their matter and of the currency scandal that had occasioned them. He had Mary fetch the book, and he read out to me a few passages of the indignant prose, holding the print within an inch of his better eye.

My father broke in at one point, starting an anecdote about the time that he and Ford had been on location in Monument Valley, when they were sitting around the campfire near the chuck wagon beating their gums, swapping stories, laughing and scratching. An old Indian who had been hired as an extra stood up and recited a poem. Nobody understood a word of it, except Dolores del Campo, who was part Indian on her mother's side, but it must have been one heck of a poem, be-cause... and here my father faltered. He covered himself with:

'Well, you know me, Jack, I'm a man of a few thousand words, but frankly, the long and the short of it was . . .'

'We can hear that one after,' Ford said.

To which my father: 'You're the director, Jack.' And Ford resumed his reading.

He told me that Swift, Dr Johnson, Fielding, and Sterne were the great masters of English prose, and the greatest of these was Swift, except for Joyce, who could write circles around anyone. He discoursed on literature for an hour or more. He showed me a book that was dedicated to him, *Famine*, by Liam O'Flaherty. I had seen *The Informer* and I asked Ford whether he was going to make a movie out of

Famine too. No, he said, he was too old, but he should have and now somebody else should. He didn't have the strength any more. It would take a strong, young man to make that picture. He filled his coffee cup with whiskey. The Irish famine was the ugliest event in the history of the western world. The English had been worse to the Irish than the Germans had been to the Jews. A picture about the famine could show just how evil people could be to one another. He took a long drink, started to doze off, and we left.

I told my father I thought Ford an extraordinary man.

'He's got a lot of bitterness in him,' my father said. 'He's one of these guys, no matter what he does, he always wants something he doesn't think he has.'

'He's an artist,' I said.

'That's right, Salty.'

I said that I was going to start reading the writers Ford had recommended right away. My father approved of this resolve, but he cautioned that I should take care not to neglect a regular program of physical exercise. He had known Scott Fitzgerald in the old days, when Fitzgerald was still a young man but ruined by alcohol:

'Died before his time, living with a woman not his wife.'

I asked him for his reminiscences about Fitzgerald.

'Sure. I knew H. L. Mencken, too. He was an atheist, you know, but very famous in his day.'

Now that we had rationalized the telephone and address book and established contact with its surviving entries, I hoped to get on with the business of cleaning up, filing away, and ordering the rest of the contents of the day room, which were as numerous as they were chaotic. But that evening, after our visit with Ford, my father grew feverish and took to his bed, complaining of pain in his eyes. He told me not to be concerned for him, that during the war he had been bitten in the eye by a rare insect in the tropics, and that from time to time the poison then injected into his system revived. I was not to call a doctor. But within a few days he was worse. It was difficult to watch him, who took such pride in his physical person, which though fat and the skin dry on it from years of exposure to the sun, was yet impressive, the legs and arms generously muscled, the neck measuring near eighteen inches around. He lay crippled up with pain, unable to rise. After a week of this, I brought in an ophthalmologist, who determined that the cornea of one eye must be removed and replaced with another. If this were not done, my father would be blind in both eyes within a few months.

He bore the surgery manfully. He bit the bullet, lying for weeks in the hospital with both eyes bandaged, with only his thoughts to occupy him. I would draw up a chair beside his bed and listen to him talk. His life was passing before him, and during those weeks he narrated the adventures of his movies, speaking often of Ford and of Duke Wayne, Harry Carey, Tom Mix, Georgie Sherman, and Mervyn Leroy, with whom he had journeyed to Mexico in a covered wagon, in the days when they starved to death together at the Hollywood YMCA. Occasionally he referred to his leading ladies, as he called them, but always with a courteous obliqueness, and as Mother had been one of these, the subject usually led back to Casa Fiesta and the rending of our family. I had written Mother about his illness and I told him that she had written back expressing concern, which cheered him, but that I had misplaced the letter, which annoyed him. In truth she had said that she hoped now he would understand a little of what suffering was and all she had gone through on account of him. She knew damned well that his veteran's benefits would pay for his operation, but what would happen to her if she got sick? The Italian doctors were all quacks, and they charged a fortune. He could count on footing the bill.

'Your Ma and I,' my father never tired of saying, 'are still married in the eyes of the Church.'

I took advantage of his confinement to pursue Linda. My

father knew about her, because he had intercepted some of her letters to me when she had been on her grand tour. I never accused him directly of reading my mail, and he never admitted it, but when he started warning me about the danger of putting things in writing and how a paternity suit could ruin a man's life, I knew what he had been up to, and I started hiding her letters under his saddle in the garage. He must have formed an unfavorable impression of her. She wrote that she might even love me and that mine were the most wonderful letters she had ever read, but mostly she described her progress across the Continent. In Copenhagen she had tasted aquavit and gravlaks with dill. The sun never set and she had met an athletic archaeology student who took her to see the people who had been dug up from bogs. He was very masculine but had long thin hands like a woman and she had not been able to resist them. In Vienna, Gumpoldskirchner, the Duc de Reichstadt's heart, an American diplomat who had followed her down the street and told her she reminded him of a girl he had once seen wading on the Jersey shore but had not had the courage to speak to. Had she eaten Sacher torte yet? He suspected his wife of sleeping with the Turkish naval attaché. He was nervous but sweet and took her everywhere, and at the Hapsburg palace she had let him put his hand under her skirt. The weather was boiling, unusual for Vienna. She liked my idea that we should be frank with each other and I could not know how much she valued writing me freely. I was becoming the best friend she had ever had, maybe something more. That was wild about Jerry Caliban and his father's mistress, but what was I up to? It wasn't fair if she was going to tell me everything. She was still confused about Marty but it was good to be away from him, he was so insistent, she felt sometimes like he was smothering her and restricting her spirit and she didn't like that at all. The beer halls in Munich were awful, smelling of stale beer and urine, but there were these four Princeton boys travelling across Europe in a Volkswagen.

They had been absolutely fantastic, the funniest guys she had ever met, and the handsomest one was heir to a pharmaceutical fortune. They had finally got off alone together and after an evening in a really *nice* bierstube she went back to his hotel room with him. She couldn't remember ever being so hot. She would have done anything. Well, boy, was he a disappointment! It looked like she had picked the wrong Princetonian. How great it would have been if he had been me. Couldn't I imagine? That would be ideal, for us to meet in some strange city and go off together. Of course we had never really done anything together, but she knew I understood why, and if we ever did, she knew it would be perfect. Maybe we were fated never to do anything, because knowing it would be so perfect was too much to bear. Maybe the thing to do was to wait for years, until we were both grown up and completely experienced and married, and then meet each other by chance. It was too dreamy to imagine. She actually got a tan in two weeks in Italy. Zermatt was so quaint, perfect for a honeymoon. In Paris she got drunk at a place that had bread in the shape of penises and so had her date and they took a crazy bath together. He was from New York but he might come out to visit her at Christmas.

I put the pressure on Linda to go out with me. It seemed a shame that we could be so close in our letters and never see each other alone. We still had lunch together, and she told me what she hadn't written of her adventures. Light and amusing she was about them, her hair fresh; I could sense the blood under her skin; other students would walk past and look at us; I was suspended in a warm cocoon of her words. Then one Wednesday she said she would be free all Friday night for me. I had put enough aside from the grocery money my father had allotted me to make a big night of it. I borrowed Jerry's fake identification, a driver's licence giving my age as 22 and my name as Caliban, and I had the DeSoto.

When I picked her up I asked her where we should have

dinner. She said she liked a man to make the decisions. Fortunately I had everything plotted out. We drove to the Amigo in Malibu and had martinis cantilevered over the surf. It was a warm October. They had the windows open and the candles fluttered. We smoked cigarettes. Linda noticed I didn't inhale and she showed me how. The smoke went to my head with the gin.

'I wish we had done this before,' I said.

'I don't like to rush things,' Linda said.

'But we've been friends since April at least.'

'I know. And you really are a friend. But you're different. You're so serious. I think it scares me a little.'

'I can be pretty funny, can't I?'

'Oh, I love your sense of humor. Your sense of humor is really unique.'

The steak was good and we had a bottle of good California red with it. I could have stayed there forever looking at her, floating over the sea. She wore a short Italian print dress that seemed hardly to touch her. Her legs were bare and her feet bare in her sandals. She was still a little tan from the summer.

'I love to drink,' she said, finishing the wine. 'Could we have a Grand Marnier?'

'Sure.'

'That's what we had the night I took the bath with that guy.'

'Do you still hate people?'

'Not now. This is a nice place. How did you find it?'

'I think my mother mentioned it.'

'Why does your mother live in Rome?'

'I don't know. She got fed up with this country.'

'And your father's in the hospital?'

'Yes.'

'Maybe we could go to your house.'

'I thought of that. But there's this jazz place I wanted you to see first. It's on the way.'

'We don't want to get too drunk.'

'That's true. We'll hear the music and have one drink. Then we'll go to my house.'

We heard Bud Shank play the tenor sax and the flute. It was a good thing we were having only one more drink because I was about broke. The music lifted us higher. I had plotted it to put her in the mood for something. It hadn't been necessary, but she liked the music and it let her see I knew my way around. I had felt she thought of me too much as a brother and I wanted to show her I was somebody who knew what to do with an evening. She sat close to me, playing with the hair on the back of my head. She was better looking and sexier than any other girl in the place. I knew that when other people looked at her they could tell she fucked and I wanted them to think we fucked each other, often.

In the DeSoto she was up against me with her arms around me as I drove. I was afraid she was falling asleep but when I pulled into our driveway she sat right up and got out. I let us in the back way and didn't turn on any lights. I took her straight into my bedroom and she turned around and kissed me with her arms around my neck. Then she took out my cock. I had the best hard-on of my life. We fell onto the bed and she helped me get her pants down and I went right into her. Her pants were still around one foot and she brought that foot up and pressed me hard under my balls, pressing me up all the way into her. We were caught fish squirming. I could feel something at the top or bottom of her that I thought was probably a diaphragm and I let myself go. When we lay there I asked her if she always wore her diaphragm. She said she didn't wear it to school, if that's what I meant. But maybe she should. Maybe she should wear it to school so we could go out to the parking lot and screw like hell during lunch hour. That would be better than lunch anyway, wouldn't it? We did it again right away. By the end of it her dress was open down the front and after it we took off the rest of our clothes and contemplated each other. Linda said she was glad I was circumcized even though I wasn't Jewish because circumcized ones felt better. The uncircumcized penis moved within itself. She took damp from herself and smoothed me with it. I told her how much I admired her frankness and I kissed her belly and breasts and took breaths of her, feeling I was breathing in wisdom and experience with the complex bouquet of her body. I told her I wished we were older and that I loved her and that this was the happiest moment of my life. She said she wanted to see the rest of the house.

I had not counted on a tour, but we stayed naked and I thought it might be fun. I could show her the house and say good-bye to it. After this how could I go on living here? I was no longer a boy, I was—someone's lover. We must have had so much in common to have found each other. I had little in common with my father, he was merely my father and not a woman anyway. I would have to find a way to get out and get money and spend every night lost in Linda. She would have much to teach me about life, she had lived a score of lives to my one. Maybe she could get money from her parents. I knew they were rich. Her father was a lawyer with big show business clients. She walked out of my room with self-sufficient grace, as though she preferred going naked. I resisted my impulse to hide from her eyes the parts that mattered of my lust glistening body. She went into the day room and I switched on the lights.

It was still a mess. We hadn't done anything since the telephone and address book.

'I thought you said your father was a movie star. This place is a pig sty.'

'I said he *was* a movie star. He hasn't worked in years. He's been pretty down since my parents' divorce. I've been trying to help out. Then he got sick.'

'That's funny,' Linda said, 'my parents would be divorced right now if it weren't for me.'

'They think it would upset you?'

'No. It's my father. He's in love with me. He doesn't want to leave me. I honestly think he'd marry me if he could. They'll get divorced when I leave. I'd bet on it.'

I could almost understand her father's feelings, looking at her. What a remarkable girl. Even her father. She was vain about her body, irresistibly vain. She stepped around the room pushing at the piles of papers with her feet. She said her parents didn't sleep together any more, hadn't for years. Her mother was having an affair with a Paramount executive. Her father didn't see anyone because he cared only for her. He bought her presents and took her out, and he had arranged the appointment for her diaphragm.

'Don't you ever get carried away,' I said, 'just looking at yourself in the mirror?'

'I'll have to try it. What's this?'

She rummaged through a cardboard box and pulled out a photograph. It was an old publicity still. It was my mother. The box was filled with glossies of her. Linda said it was sick for my father to keep this stuff around. When something was over, it was over. It was very sad, but it was over. I said that one day I hoped he would get over it but maybe he never would.

'He should get married again,' Linda said.

'He says he can't because he's Catholic.'

'It's sick.'

'I don't understand it either,' I said.

She said her father would never marry again, but that was because he loved her. My mother was very beautiful. Did she still look like that?

'Sort of.'

'What color hair did she have?'

'Red.'

'Do you like red hair?'

'I've never liked a girl with red hair. I like your hair.'

I wanted to get off the subject of my parents. I was getting depressed.

'It's lighter when I'm in the sun. Do you like the rest of me?'

She looked down at herself, holding the photograph away from her. She was near a chair and she put one foot up on the seat of it.

FIFTEEN

The Beach

My father was glad to give an eye for his country. Other men had made the ultimate sacrifice, and he was proud that the Government was paying for the operation, which was a complete success. His left eye was now that of a twenty-five-year-old female with a social conscience killed on the freeway, and so fiercely did the male eye compete with the female, that it discovered strength, matching youth in brightness. My father was of the opinion that half a century of intelligent care for his body, not discounting the grace of God, had made possible this rejuvenation. In the history of medicine I can think of no more apt an analogy than the effect of the Steinmetz monkey gland operation on the poet Yeats. In my father's case no bawdy lyrics resulted, nor any increase in sexual desire, so far as I could see; but in genital matters, my father kept himself to himself, and I could neither read his thoughts nor know the dreams that gave him torment or delight.

Eagerly he joined me in ordering the day room. I had nothing better to do. The rest of my night of love with Linda had not gone so well. She said I was just like all the others. Then she took that back. It was true that I seemed to know and understand what a girl felt, that was what attracted her to me in the first place, and my letters proved that it was so. But I was too young and inexperienced, that was probably the real problem. She had not planned to tell me this, but she and Marty were engaged to be married. He was graduating from

U.C.L.A. this year and they would be married in a big ceremony at the Bel-Air Hotel. There were already 300 guests on the list including Danny Kaye, who was going to do a routine especially for them. Her father would put Marty through law school and Marty's father was going to help out too. Marty's father was a shoe manufacturer with outlets from coast to coast. But I shouldn't get the idea that any of this meant that she was giving up her freedom. She would always be Linda and she would always be free. She told me these things parked outside her house early in the morning. I had an idea I could talk her out of it given enough time, but she said that light meant her father was waiting up for her and would want to talk. He confided everything to her. When I got home I kicked in a window but I replaced the glass before my father got out of the hospital.

My father commented on each photograph of my mother: the circumstance of its exposure; the professional history of its photographer; the public reaction to its appearance in whatever magazine, newspaper, or publicity vehicle; the facets of beauty and character emphasized by it. One in particular, showing my mother in sable-trimmed, leopardskin cape and platform shoes, hair banged and crowned with a Spanish comb, eyes intently bold, mouth heavily lipsticked and faintly curled, curved fingernails lifting the fur's nap, pleased him.

'That one belongs on the wall, Salty, don't you think?'

'Strictly up to you, Dad.'

'I remember it well. It was a marathon session, but I kept the car waiting. Then we headed for the Grove. We danced all night, rhumbas, sambas, your mother was a great dancer, she was a great kid in those days. Rick Cortez was there and we ended up out at the beach house at five in the morning. When the sun came up we all hit the water. Nothing like the surf after a big night. *Huevos rancheros*, flapjacks, the works. And how about five sets of tennis? That's right. Your Ma didn't play tennis. A great horse-woman, though. We used to ride along the beach, before the motels and the supermarkets.'

'That was some life,' I said.

'Hey,' my father said, 'I've got an idea. Tell you what it is. When we knock off today, we grab our trunks and a couple of towels and head for the beach. How's that?'

'Fine.' My father was taut with enthusiasm.

'And we'll call up old Marsh and see if he wants to come along.'

I tacked up the photograph next to a framed letter from Admiral Arleigh '30 Knots' Burke, Naval Commandant, later Chairman of the Joint Chiefs of Staff, commending my father for service beyond the call of duty for his participation in a Fourth of July pageant honoring John Paul Jones and Commodore Perry.

I had not seen Marshall since our story conference, as my father's illness had delayed follow up meetings, and there had been no meetings scheduled since. At the beach Marshall kept his shirt on. He was self-conscious about his battle scars, my father explained.

'Let's hit the water.'

We plunged in and rode the waves together as of old, my father hurling himself shoulder-first into a breaker, hollering, exulting, swimming again, skimmed along, floating, thrashing father, alive, confident as waves. Hero. We caught some beauties, and Dad was pleased I had not forgotten the body-surfing skills he had imparted to me. He did complain that I was underweight and needed filling out if I was going to develop my stamina. As for him, how old did I think he looked? I told him he could pass for a man in his mid-forties. In truth he looked to me both older and younger than he was, nearing sixty. The fat made him younger and the muscles were awesome, but, lying next to him on the beach, I noted the spots and crinkles of age. He had plenty of hair left, but I had discovered a bottle of dye in his desk during one of my private inventories.

If he reached seventy, he would try to look sixty. Youth meant everything to him.

Marshall was in a bad way. His ex-wife was taking him to court about the alimony. He didn't have the money, and he knew that she could throw him in jail. For a man who had done so much for his country to end up in its jails seemed unjust. There ought to be a fund for divorced war heroes. And automobile sales were slumping. This was because of commie propaganda, of course, but short of a military takeover, he didn't see what could be done about it. They ought to lob one into the men's room of the Kremlin. It was the same with this tobacco cancer scare thing. That was a bold-faced attempt to undermine the economy of the South by so-called scientist dupes. He was going to do a novena.

My father asked me later had I got the impression that old Marsh was trying to touch him for a loan. I said that it had occurred to me and that if I had any money I would probably give him some. My father said that this was the wrong approach, that you never helped a man by trying to make things easy for him. You had to pay your own way, that was the only way you learned a lesson in life. Marsh would learn, and if he had to go to jail, well, everything in life taught a lesson, and if he was a real man, he would come out the stronger for it. I told my father that I knew a girl whose father loved her so much that he was going to pay for her husband's education and support them until they could make it on their own. My father said that was the worst thing in the world and it would only breed trouble. The first time those young people hit rough water and old Dad wasn't around to bail them out, they'd have to find out the hard way. He had seen people like that split up. People who came up the hard way together stayed together. I tried to take some satisfaction from this. Maybe in fifteen years I would run into Linda coming out of her psychiatrist's or her lawyer's office. I envied Marty his ten or fifteen years with her, but maybe I would get her in the end. I thought about her all the time, but at school I found it difficult to speak to her, she was so godamned lighthearted.

In the old days secretaries had dealt with Dad's fan mail. Now it ran to half a dozen letters a year, and these he had undertaken to answer himself. But he had fallen about five years behind, so I assisted him in working through the correspondence. Seven of the outstanding letters proved to be from one person, the wife of the dean of a small college in Illinois. The seventh letter inquired whether he was dead. She would cease pestering him if this were the case. She wanted an autographed picture to add to her scrapbook of his life. As a young girl in Los Angeles, she had seen all of his movies. She used to stand outside the Hollywood Athletic Club waiting for a glimpse of him as he emerged from a morning workout. He had given her an autograph in 1938, but he probably wouldn't remember. She had hundreds of clippings. She had a shot of my parents on their wedding day. That had broken her teenage heart, but even then she had wished him every happiness. At my father's dictation I sent this letter to her:

Dear Mrs Voelkel,

Thank you very much for your kind letters, which I have been unable to answer owing to pressing business. I have a number of deals on the fire, and you know how it is with these Hollywood people. They keep at you. I am delighted that you and your husband are involved out there in education, because there is nothing as important to our youth today. My son, Salty, is very involved in education himself and will soon be going to college. I never went to college myself, although I have often regretted it, because you can't beat education. But instead I chose the road to adventure in the pioneer days of Hollywood, and I've never looked back. Thank God I also had the opportunity to serve my country in the United States Navy, and it isn't many men who have had two careers. But my greatest career has been my wife and son. Please convey my best regards to your husband, and keep up the good work out there in Illinois. I enclose an autographed photo, so you can keep your scrapbook up to date.

He had stacks of these pictures, which I filed for future use. In them he was pensive, menacing, grinning, wistful, his head thrown back in a careless laugh; in cowboy garb, dinner jacket, boxing trunks, plus fours, football gear, stripped hurling a discus. For Mrs Voelkel he chose a shot of himself in Lieutenant Commander's uniform, gazing out to sea through binoculars.

Many of the other letters were from the Orient. Over these we labored carefully, for my father reminded me of many strange customs in that part of the world and of the obligation of the Westerner not to offend. The American especially must remember that he travels always as a representative of his country.

Mrs Voelkel's scrapbook gave me the idea of compiling one of our own, a master scrapbook out of the scrapheap. My father welcomed the suggestion. In public life you ought to have a scrapbook, because the pressure of time and events is such that you could be caught off guard when the biographers came along, not knowing which end was up. He guessed, although a writer's projects were his own business and under international copyright, that someday I might undertake myself to write his biography. In my spare time maybe. He owed it to his public and to me to see that all the material was there. In cases like this only a scrapbook stood between you and a pack of lies. If someone came along and said such and such was so, or your father was a rotten so and so, you could pull out the scrapbook and give them the facts. I got clippings to prove it, you could say.

He made proud use of his new vision, rereading each clipping with naked eyes. He kept the chronology straight. He corrected or elaborated. Without him I could never have completed the task. For convenience I followed standard library practice in binding periodicals, with a separate volume for each year, each indexed. In the later volumes we left many empty pages, so we would have room for material that might turn up later. I found an announcement of my birth in Ed Sullivan's column.

SIXTEEN

Self-Deception

The telephone.

'Hello, dear. Don't die of shock. It's your old mother.'

It had been two years since I had spoken to her. She sounded very close.

'Of course not. You think I'd be calling from Europe at those prices? You ought to have your head examined. I'm right here in dear old L.A. I'm staying with Maggie and Sterling. They were sweethearts to put me up. Sterling isn't well, poor thing. You wouldn't recognize him.'

She had no special reason for coming except that prices in Rome had gone sky high and she had to figure out a way to live within her income. I had calculated that what she had left from the divorce settlement gave her about $15,000 a year, better than a Sicilian linguini farmer anyway. Times were tough all over. I had done quite a lot of calculating lately. I had decided that I was better off manning my battle station on my father's flagship than I would be running with her again. For one thing, there was no telling what the new Anatol might be like. I wanted out of the next losing proposition.

It was Thanksgiving again. She had a swell idea but she wanted to discuss it with me first before I mentioned it to my father. Maggie had offered to fix a turkey. Mother would do a plum pudding and I could fix the hard sauce. It would be just like old times.

'Plum pudding is for Christmas, Mother,' I said.

'Oh what the hell difference does it make! Use your little genius brain. Here I'm making a perfectly decent suggestion. Do you think your father will come?'

'You're inviting him?'

'Of course I'm inviting him. That is if he can be civilized.'

Just like old times. What was up? Had she found the new Anatol already? Gigolo sounded like an Italian word. Darlings, I want you to meet Paulo. He doesn't understand a word of English so you're free to tell me he's the most beautiful boy you've ever seen.

'I think,' I said, 'Dad was planning to invite Marshall Marshall over here.'

'Who in God's name is Marshall Marshall?'

'Never mind. I'll ask Dad. I'll let you know how he feels.'

'Well don't take forever. We have to do the shopping. If he wants to accept my gesture, fine. If not, to hell with him.'

I postponed telling my father. I considered calling her back and offering to meet her on neutral ground, say a church. I told myself I ought to be more excited about seeing her, but I felt dreadful. I wanted more from her than a turkey. I conveyed her message.

'Your Ma and I have been married twenty-five years,' my father said, 'and every year I learn something new. That's what makes life interesting. If you stop learning, you're dead. You know that because you're a student of life yourself.'

My inquiries into human understanding had taught me that my father was as constantly constant as a rock and my mother as constantly inconstant as the sea, and that wasn't much to go on. A rock as big as my father you could not throw, but you could hide behind it and rest in its shadow. When it fell into the sea, it sank.

'I'm not sure how the evening would turn out,' I said. 'It could be all right, and then again it couldn't.'

'All you know from one day to the next is that the sun will shine, unless it's raining. You can't predict what a woman will do, and your mother is a woman, Salty. Maybe she's finally come to her senses.'

'How?'

'Maybe she finally realizes what a mistake she made.'

'It's possible. I sort of doubt it.'

'I wouldn't of married her if I thought she was all crazy, and she wasn't. If I knew then what I know now, I wouldn't have gone away to World War II.'

'She's done some pretty erratic things. I don't think she's been very fair to you.'

'You can't expect fairness. Tell me, Salty. You're getting to be a man. Did you ever think your Ma had a little of the lesbian in her?'

'I never thought of that,' I said. 'It's a possibility.' Here was something new. I remembered Mother telling me about the time a certain famous actress had made a pass at her on a yacht. They were lying off Catalina and all of a sudden the woman's hand was where it oughtn't have been. Mother said this showed why the woman liked playing Rosalind. Did my father have any evidence?

'I'm not saying it against her,' he said, 'but some people have problems. The time she brought two fags around. I tell you, if we ever got together again, I'd put a stop to that. No more fags. I think she thought it was fashionable or some kind of a thing. She brought these two fags around, and it turned out they wanted my picture. Can you beat that? They were fans of mine. Hell, I got nothing against fags. But I got out of there. I hadda get busy.'

'What are you going to do about the invitation?'

'I look at it this way. I got plenty of reasons for not going, right? Some you know, some you don't know. Maggie, for instance, turned against me in the divorce. You don't know this, but she was your mother's witness. She told a lot of lies, son, and I don't forget it. Can you imagine? She told the judge that I didn't care about a home and family. Said I came back from the war and didn't care about my wife and son any more. That really hurt. You know I'm the greatest family man that ever was.'

'I know that.'

'And it ruined my career, too. That's what ruined my career. It was all over the papers. That she was divorcing me because I didn't love my family any more. That was the biggest lie ever told. Are you with me?'

'Yes.'

'So I got my reasons. But nobody ever accused me of being small. I leave that to the others. So if you ask me am I going to accept this invitation, I say, why not, I'm a big enough guy to forgive and forget, and there's one other thing, let it never be said that I wouldn't do anything for my family.'

He slept little before the Thursday. He got out all his old clothes and brushed them and tried them on. He asked me whether he ought to go in uniform but I said I thought civvies were in order. He was up one minute and depressed the next. Entirely out of character, he brought home a bottle of beer that we shared, man to man. He had stomach troubles, malaria coming back, he said, and paced around the house in his underwear farting a lot.

'You look marvellous,' Mother said to him as she opened the door. 'Good God, I always knew you'd bury us all. Hello, my darling boy. It's so wonderful to see you.'

We kissed and she held onto me. There was a boozy odor. She seemed to have shrunk. She held me and then looked at me at arm's length and held me again.

Sterling was unable to get out of his chair but was otherwise unchanged. Maggie gave my father a showbiz hug:

'You old son of a bitch. I could get you a part right now.'

'I'm all tied up in a couple of deals,' my father said. 'There's this war picture and a TV thing I'm working on. Coupla fellas doing an underwater thing. I know the ropes.'

I accepted a martini from Sterling, who had everything set up beside his chair. My father had a coke. Mother's drink was invisible.

'You off the sauce?' I said to her.

She cast me an eye of hurt shock.

'As a matter of fact I am,' she said, very queenly. 'It's not easy to admit you're an alcoholic, but I've done it. I've joined A.A. in Rome. We have a wonderful chapter of Americans.'

'I'm proud of you,' my father said. 'It's a step in the right direction.'

Mother talked about A.A. for the next fifteen minutes. We heard about the pledge and the steps to sobriety and not taking a drink this one day. The people in real trouble would telephone her at all hours and she would talk them out of that fatal first gulp. God played a role. It had been so long now since she had had a drink, she wasn't even tempted any more, or hardly ever. In A.A. you formed enduring friendships. Alcoholism was a disease, like diabetes or an allergy. Some people got puffed up if they ate nuts. She regretted having to miss so many A.A. meetings being over here. She could go to a local chapter but her real friends were in Rome now.

'It's too bad,' I said. 'Drinking is a part of life, isn't it? I mean drinking and getting drunk. Making an ass of yourself. Even making things unpleasant for other people. It's too bad if you can't do that any more. I would feel very deprived if I thought I couldn't do that for the rest of my life.'

'I don't know what you're talking about,' Mother said. 'You're very young.'

'A.A. sounds very boring to me,' I said. 'It sounds like some half-assed evangelical sect. People sitting around talking about not drinking. Why not tie one on and go to sleep?'

'People do terrible things to their lives,' Mother said. 'You don't know the half of it.'

'I'll bet they do.'

'I don't like your tone,' Mother said. 'I can see they aren't teaching you manners in school. I think you should start on the hard sauce, don't you? It needs to be chilled.'

I could hear the conversation from the kitchen as I mashed the butter and the sugar together and added the rum, taking a few slugs when I was sure no one was looking. Sterling was upset. An entire grove of his avocados had been wiped out by cinnamon root rot. The trouble was, once the cinnamon root rot struck, you could never grow avocados in the same place again. The rot struck all avocado trees eventually, but this had been a young grove. Property values were up, and he didn't know how he was going to buy another plot suitable for avocados. I took more rum and conjured millions of arable square miles rot-blighted and billion dollar desert irrigation schemes. Man's lust for avocados would be satisfied. Linda would be sitting down at Perino's with her father and Marty. I was under the table with my head between her knees. I mashed away and I began to feel omnipotent and I took more rum. I filled my mouth full, let it trickle down, and stuffed butter and sugar in after. If I could get through this dinner I was going to go out tomorrow and find some sexy bitch who wasn't hung up on her father and the scion of shoe millions. Linda could fucking well go to hell. My father said Sterling's story reminded him of Okinawa.

'Christ spare us Okinawa,' Mother said.

I liked my mother for the moment. Maybe my father had driven her to drink and other pricks out of boredom. But he couldn't have been the same then. He was a star. She had ruined him. She had snipped off his balls and eaten them. Who knew or cared? I had my own life. She was as unhappy as he was, wasn't she? Maybe he could take satisfaction from that some day. If he could survive her he might enjoy watching her lowered.

When I rejoined the pow-wow Mother said she could always count on me to make the hard sauce at holiday time. No one could say I wasn't good for something. I was a top-notch first mate, my father said. That was the first I had heard of my promotion and I took another martini to celebrate.

Raising my glass, 'Here's to Mother,' I said. 'May she die in Hollywood.'

'I'm not sure I appreciate the sentiment,' Mother said.

'Don't be silly,' I said. 'It's a hallowed toast. All the old buggers say it.'

My father and I carried Sterling to the table. He couldn't carve sitting down so my father volunteered. He botched it and Mother let him know it.

'I was thinking of asking you how you felt about living together again but after watching you hack away at that thing I don't know if I could stand it.'

My father looked at her not knowing whether to take heart or umbrage. Was this the person living in his mind?

'The Italian butchers are marvelous,' Mother said. 'They're actually aesthetic about meat. But that's the way they are about everything. The flowers, the wine. I have never seen an Italian drunk. There was a horrible American drunk on the plane. He ruined the trip for everybody.'

'You'd know something about that,' I said.

'About what?'

'Nothing. Ruined trips. You've travelled so widely.'

'Jesus Christ,' Mother said, 'I'm sick of travelling. I want to find a place and settle down for once. That's what I've always wanted.'

'Have some more white meat,' my father said. 'You'd better have some more white meat and some stuffing, too.'

'Did he vomit?' I asked my mother.

'What? Who?'

'Better have some stuffing,' my father said, 'there's plenty cranberry sauce.'

'The drunk American on the plane. Did he vomit? Did he get to the bag in time?'

'You're being disgusting,' Mother said. 'You're embarrassing me in front of Maggie and Sterling.'

'I just want to get the facts straight. Did he vomit, and if so, did he vomit on you? If not, how did he ruin the trip? I don't like these vague accusations. Maybe he didn't ruin the trip at all. Maybe he made the trip a memorable experience for everyone. It can get pretty boring on a plane. I was so bored coming back from Paris that time I had to go into the john to beat off.'

Mother started to cry. I got up from the table and went outside. I was sweating, my head was swimming, I took deep breaths of the cool air. I picked up a rock and hurled it against a tree. It was a good throw and it calmed me down. I went in and apologized. I felt like stuffing my mother's head in the turkey.

'I don't know why the Americans have to have turkey,' Mother said, quite recovered. 'Nobody else eats it. You wouldn't find an Italian eating turkey on a holiday. They have more imagination. But their desserts all taste the same, and the bread is lousy. Of course American bread is the worst. It's why everyone in this country looks so terrible.'

'Everyone is on a diet,' Maggie said. 'It's all the crap they eat.'

'I noticed it right away when I got off the plane,' Mother said, and to Dad: 'You wouldn't be so fat if you lived in Italy. If the day ever comes when we live together again, you can be sure I won't live here. Certainly not in Los Angeles. Maybe New York.'

'My contacts are here,' my father said. 'I can't let people down.'

'Oh horseshit,' Mother said. 'You never let that bother you.'

'I guess I'm the heavy,' my father said.

'Forgive me, but when you've lived alone as long as I have, you tend to forget some people can't stand the truth. Oh my God, I've forgotten the plum pudding! You see!'

She upset her chair and lurched into the kitchen. It was only a canned pudding but she had not put it into boiling water yet.

It would be half an hour before I would pour brandy over it, fire it, and carry it in to gasps. Maggie talked about Zanuck. Sterling put his head down to conserve energy. My father got to Okinawa. Mother asked me had I heard about Anatol.

'It's too tragic. He had another stroke. He's completely paralyzed from the neck down. I can't bear to go see him, not at this stage in my life. They have him strapped to a table. Would you go see him for me, dear?'

I refused. What had he ever done for me? He was her problem. She berated my cruelty, coldness, and heartlessness. Here was a man who had shown me love. Didn't I know that he had included me in his will? I was to get the statues of my choice. She was to get the studio and selling it would help her get through another year, if she lived that long. She went on. I would have to live with my heartlessness the rest of my life. She appealed to my father. Had he been turning me against her?

'I've never said a word against you,' he said. 'You're the mother of my son.'

'I don't know,' Mother said. 'You struggle all your life. You try to give love. Certainly I've made mistakes. But.'

A little bell sounded in the kitchen. Mercifully it was pudding time. Mother got up to fetch it and closed the kitchen door behind her so she could get at the rum bottle.

We heard her rattling around and weeping softly. My father started to get up to go comfort her. He opened the kitchen door and we watched as she removed the can from the boiling water and set it down.

'Can I help?' my father said.

'I don't need any help, thank you.'

She jabbed the can with an opener and the pudding blew up in her face. She had neglected to put an air hole in the can before she boiled it. The pudding burst like a small bomb and jetted up at her, covering her face with boiling ooze. She screamed and fell writhing and screaming. My father was at her

126

side calling for ice before the rest of us had moved. Sterling woke up and passed out. Maggie brought the ice bucket and my father bathed the blistering face with ice and water. We put her into the DeSoto and I drove to the hospital with my father in the rear cradling his wife.

We were back in two hours. The doctors pointed out that it had been the U.S. Navy that had discovered the homeostatic principle of the application of ice to burns. Butter was out. The ice had made all the difference. If it hadn't been for the war, my mother's face might have been ruined. She looked pretty awful, patchy with ointment and dying skin, and she was more angry at what had happened than grateful that it could have been worse. Nothing went right for her here. She was going to move to Spain. She was fed up with this country. I had certainly been no help. She didn't know what I wanted out of life but she hoped that I would get it and that I realized what sort of price I would pay for it. I was not what you would call a lovable child. I scarcely wrote her. I didn't know what love was and she pitied the girl who got stuck with me. What did I want from her anyway? She would go to Spain to be with her old friend Donna Esmeralda Cordova the famous female bull-fighter from the 'thirties who was married to a duke. They had wonderful doctors in Spain because they had to treat so many bull gorings.

And other psycho-social observations. I would have to go on listening. Everyone would, everyone always did. I wanted to say no, I will not listen any more, you ought to be put in a cage and shipped off to New Guinea to be eaten. I had to face it, she had failed to live up to my assumptions, and there was some doubt that I would ever forgive her for that. It was better to assume nothing. This wreck my mother, how did I know what had gone into her that I had come out of her? I didn't look anything like him, I was probably prop man's spawn, bastard sprout of her vegetable cook, or had Don Enrique given it to her good, floor of the tack room, bedding of saddle blankets smelling of mare's lather, old man's seed tequila-watery, bang, boom, miracle of life, timing is everything, ladies and gentlemen, the secret of comic delivery, a star is born. Why was my father standing solicitous listening, patient gelding, spur accepting, animal faithful? More ointment, dear, I think a little more ointment will do the trick. Make her take a spoonful of ointment every hour, that'll do the trick. The scars still on her wrists, *there* was a failure of nerve we will pay for forever, *there* was a chance for salvation missed. Greatest act of self-sacrifice since Christ, heaven rolls out red carpet. Think of it, a bribed coroner, a box office funeral, premature passing mourned, known to family and intimates she had been ill for some time, leaves ex-husband, ex-son, and memories too numerous. In lieu of flowers donations please to the Motion Picture Relief Fund. A new life then, Dad back on the boards, Anatol happy with his whores. No, no, this was not my mother, this was what was left of her. You could still see the other mother, she had all her teeth, she kept her nails almond-perfect. Look hard, I told myself, what you see is suffering, will yourself to pity. She means no harm. She is finished, that's definite, felled by a pudding.

SEVENTEEN

Mulholland Drive

I decided I was becoming more self-reliant. I had a record player now and a few jazz records, and I would shut myself up in my room and play them for hours. I had a tin whistle too. I would play along with the music trying to make my tin whistle sound like an alto saxophone. Sometimes I would get carried away by the music and dance like crazy in my room, and if my father was out I would sing and shout, leaping around, springing from the bed and pushing off from the ceiling. There was pure exultation in soaring sound, the celebration of daring sound dancing. The sound was in me but also just before me, leading me out. The sound told me I could dance and sing, and the sound told me to write poetry. When I wrote the poems and read them over and over they were terrible, never as real and free as the music, but I went on writing them for a while and playing the music. It would stay in my head and lighten my day.

Oh I had a future. It was 1955 and I had a future. The girls, the women I was to meet were nowhere within sight but I had a future. There would be one girl, I knew it, the music told me it, my heart told me it, whom I would love like the beach and the ocean in the far off days of ease. And wouldn't I go to a fine university? That would change things, that would make all the difference. I got a great kick filling out the applications. I was filling out my future. Harvard asked for an account of a typical week. What a week I wrote of! When I wasn't in school I was reading Dostoevsky, playing chess or baseball or going to mass or fulfilling my duties as president of the boys' honor society. Harvard wanted a list of the books I had read in the last year, too. Such a list, such powers of invention did I discover within myself, that list was a work of art. For Princeton I wrote of my most memorable experience. I did a draft on my grandmother's funeral, with appropriate quotations on death, but rejected it for my reactions to American Legion Boys' State. They had bedded us down in cattle stalls at the Sacramento Fair Grounds. A future farmer had been elected governor, and we had toured the capitol and seen a million dollars in cash. I had hated it, but I wrote of how wonderful it had been and how I couldn't wait to vote. A smash essay. But Jerry Caliban's was even better. For him I wrote how seeing Olivier's *Hamlet* had made him read all of Shakespeare twice. He took me out to dinner for it. He was as anxious to get away to college as I was. Mrs Caliban was in an institution now.

I had been nearly two years caring for my father and had some reason to be pleased with my work. His habits were again cleanly, his house and its treasures were in order, his spirits were level, except for the periodic fit of gloom, which he often tried to conceal from me. Behind the door of his room he would pace, sigh, and say prayers to himself. I would try to cheer him up with jokes or by preparing a good meal, though like sheep, who are very subject to the rot if their pasture is too succulent, he thrived on the simplest fare. Thinking of my future made it easier to carry out my responsibilities, and I cooked also out of selfishness, because he was eccentric in the kitchen, and like many who have suffered a reverse of fortune, he was too concerned with economy. Left to himself, he would buy the cheapest cut of meat, apply a chemical tenderizer to it and broil it the next day, when it was mush. He would cover the mush with cottage cheese and canned pineapple and offer it as Steak Oahu: Duke Kahanamoko had confided the recipe to him after a heavy day of surfing. A fellow needed plenty of protein to manage the seventy pound redwood boards they used in the old days.

My father had taken to watering the milk in the interests of economy, but the practice did nothing to improve the flavor. I had never actually observed him doing this, but the milk had become unpalatable, and the O-So-Cool kept it lukewarm. One evening, after he had asked me for the sixth time why I was not drinking my milk, with attendant remarks on the role of calcium in the building of bones, I explained that I preferred the drink in its natural state, with only such adulterations as were required by law for the prevention of disease.

'Salty, sometimes I think you read too many books.'

'I don't care for milk with water in it,' I said. 'Some drinks benefit from the addition of water, but milk isn't one of them. Why don't we leave the water for coffee and tea?'

'Drink it,' he said. 'On the double. Stop lolly-gagging.'

I shook my head.

'I'm giving you an order, mister. This is an order from your Commander-in-Chief!'

I drained the glass and effortlessly brought the liquid up again, covering the table. My father was around to my chair in a second, lifting me out by the seat of my pants. I weighed at the time about a hundred and fifty pounds, but he held me aloft by one hand, shaking me and shouting into my face:

'You are the most ungrateful snot-nosed little bastard I ever saw!'

This was for him strong language, and I quaked, dangling. He told me that if I had any guts, I would step outside and fight him like a man. The folly of that course was obvious. He would have destroyed me. Though in all my life he had never lifted a hand against me, I saw that his frenzy called for guile.

'Let's go, sailor,' he said. 'We're having it out.' He propelled me towards the back yard.

'Stop!' I said, a wriggling puppet come to life. 'I'll call the newspapers! So help me, I will, I'll call the newspapers! That

would look great, wouldn't it? ACTOR BEATS SON TO
PULP.'

Immediately I uttered these words I regretted them because
he could have used the publicity. I recalled how actors profited
by notoriety, how legends were born of violence, bankruptcy,
indecent exposure. Americans, moreover, were in revolt
against permissive child rearing. Juvenile crime was up, dope
addiction spreading, long hair around the corner. By making
an example of me, Dad would be a hero to millions. Why did
you beat your son to a pulp? I'm worried about this country.
(Cheers, applause.) I was perplexed. I would rehabilitate my
father and be crippled for life.

But he dropped me. I hurried to my room, where I remained
some hours, until he came quietly to me, requesting a man-to-
man talk. He discoursed on the chain of command, how vital it
was to any operation, in business, in religion, in war; how some
things were in my department, some in his; how he had seen
young men, many of them still in their 'teens, some of them
Catholics, mowed down by enemy fire, simply because they
had disobeyed their commanding officer, trying to take a beach
before the signal was given and the heavy Navy guns could be
trained on Jap emplacements; how his own father, a policeman, had taught him the lesson early on, knocking him cold
under the stove when he had stepped out of line. I told my
father that I saw his point and that he had greater experience of
life than I.

'I can save you so many scars, Salty,' he said, 'if you'll just
listen to me. Listen to the old man. He's been around.'

He put his arms around me and hugged me.

'You may not think much of me now,' he said, 'but we had a
hell of a life, your Ma and me, I'm not kidding. Look at those
scrapbooks. See us at the Riviera. See us here and there. See us
in Panama. I came back from the war. A lot of guys didn't come
back. A lot of them were dead, sure, but you know about the
missing in actions. M.I.A.'s. I tell you, a lot of those guys just

disappeared because they didn't want to come back. They had family problems, wife trouble. I met a character out in China, he said to me, why should I leave? Why should I go back to that? Look, I'm fed up to here with that broad. These people are nice to me. Ding-how. Poco-poco. See what I mean?'

'Sure,' I said.

'But I came back. And boy did I get murdered. But I have no regrets. What's resentment? What for?'

'I think that's wise,' I said.

'You understand, sure. Maybe you can understand something else. Maybe it's wrong, but you know, when that happened to your mother with that dessert, remember?'

'Yes.'

'When that happened with that dessert, I took care of everything, you know? If it hadn't of been for me, well you know what I'm talking about. Old Sterling there, he wasn't much help. But you know, when I was there with your mother, trying to help her face, showing the training I went through, it did cross my mind, maybe there's such a thing as retribution.'

'I have to go out,' I said.

'Sure. Permission granted. You want the keys?'

He reached into his pocket and brought out the keys, but he didn't give them to me. This was a way he had of prolonging a conversation. He would keep something that I needed so he could go on talking. I held out my hand for the keys but he stepped back a pace.

'I've fought back,' he said, 'but sometimes it gets to me and I have to fight it. Do you ever have hallucinations?'

'I don't think so.'

'I've had hallucinations. I tell you, I used to be a great guy for the morning. Morning was the best time. I'd jump out of the sack and hit the deck ready to go fifteen rounds. Now I wake up about four and just lie there. It's pretty rough. I dread getting up sometimes. And then these hallucinations come into my room. I'll hear a noise outside the window. Or I feel a hand on my shoulder. Men and women standing around the bed. They want to get at me. I keep the six-gun under the bed and sometimes I pick it up and wave it at them and they go away.'

'You don't want to fire it. You want to be careful, Dad.'

'No, no, I don't fire it. And I know they're hallucinations. But I need something to threaten them. They usually go away when I wave the gun. I know they're hallucinations but I have to get rid of them somehow. Puts me in a sweat. If they don't go away they start closing in on me. Did you ever hear me screaming in the morning?'

'No.'

'Good. You're a sound sleeper, just like I was. I slept through an earthquake when everybody thought it was the end of the world. But not any more. I've got to fight this thing. I know you want to shove off. You want the keys?'

'Thanks.'

'Here.'

I tore out of the driveway. I drove to Linda's house but Marty's car was parked outside. I drove to Jerry's but nobody was home. I drove up into the hills past parked couples and found a lonely spot to look at the city.

Avenues of creeping headlights, strings of streetlamps, lighted houses sheltering people. All those lives, I knew nothing of them. How many of those streets had I driven, my father before me, my mother and father before me, passing unnoticed and not noticing? What if I had been born into that house or that, my father would play the violin, and would my mother sew? But he was pensioned off and she had diabetes. My father was waiting up for me. Fallen star my father, hole in the firmament, no more than a heavenly element does he know why he has fallen, meteor innocent. His telephone silent, his private number up. Maybe I could drive to San Diego and back before morning. I had two dollars. I could have breakfast at a truck stop, mingle with real people. I started off hyped up, future impatient, but by the time I got to Hermosa Beach I was tired and bored, and I turned around and went home.

We embarked on an intensive program of physical fitness. I needed to build up my strength for college, my father said, and for a man who had once appeared semi-nude on the cover of Bernarr McFadden's *Physical Culture* magazine, he was out of shape. He had me feel his bicep, which was so large that I could not join the fingers of both my hands around it, and punch him in the stomach, which though bulging was invulnerable. He worried that I had become stooped, round-shouldered, and crook-backed, and that I would not be capable of standing at attention properly, when the time came for me to fulfill my obligation to my country. He told me that fame and fortune were nothing, if you hadn't your health.

I thought I would go along. I liked the idea of being strong, and maybe we could share something, but it was punishment. He established a daily routine: up at six, a cold shower to get the circulation going, off to the Beverly Hills Club. He had been a member of this place since 1928, though he had not visited it since the war, and he was pleased that some of the locker and steam room attendants remembered him. When they asked where he had been all these years, my father said that he was not at liberty to divulge the full nature of his activities, but that he had been doing some work for the Government, including a mission to the Far East, and that we were in danger of going soft, as Americans. When millions of Chinee and other Asian peoples were subsisting on a bowl of rice a week, we had steak and potatoes every night. But as long as there were a few fellows around willing to stay up late and watch out for the rest, we might get by, if we woke up and got off our duffs. His father had taught him to live in the present. You couldn't look back, and you couldn't go back on life. After all the wars he had come back from, things were looking pretty down hill and shady, which was an old cowboy saying.

This was his son, Salty. Salty was still a lightweight, but he would fill out soon.

'We're going to make a champ out of him, isn't that right, Salty?'

I thought the prospect of my becoming so much as a ranked contender unlikely. I asked were we to swim that morning.

'We'll leave that to Vic here,' my father said. 'Vic's the best in the business. Vic's trained a lot of champions.'

Vic was the most ancient of the attendants. He had cauliflower ears, a damaged nose, and white hair all over his body. He never spoke, and I do not know whether he was capable of speech, but he emitted a high laugh, a sort of giggle, and my father understood him perfectly.

We began by skipping rope, then, at a signal from Vic, some work on the heavy bag, then the light bag. Of these I enjoyed most the rope skipping, which I was able to manage with some grace. But the heavy bag was too heavy for me to make any impression on it, and the light bag was too light for me to keep up with it, as it whacked back and forth in a blur, popping me in the face. Nor was I much good at the sparring. For this we wore twelve-ounce gloves, and after a minute I found it difficult to keep my hands above my waist. My father assured me that as I was left-handed by nature, I would have a substantial advantage fighting out of a right-hand stance: the strength of my left jab would be such a shock to my opponent that he would never recover from it, and I could finish him off with my right. Yet my jab proved only fair, and as I had no strength at all in my right arm, my attack had neither surprise nor reserve power to it, and I saw very early that my climb to the championship would be a long one.

The main business complete, we took to the swimming pool. While my father slipped easily up and down, using a stroke he said he had taught Johnny Weissmuller, keeping his head at all times above the surface, his great arms drawing him along, I spent most of my time underwater, saying I was practising my breathing, in truth trying to stave off collapse. Ahead lay the steam room, which for me had all the attractions of the rack or the gibbet: shortness of breath and such instruction in the sadness of life's course as the sight of scars, boils, and shriveled parts can provide. My father enjoyed a steam. It was necessary, he said, to prevent tightening of the muscles. We sat there sweating together.

A couple of weeks of this routine and I noticed some improvement in my stamina. I never landed a punch, but I was able to keep my hands up till the bell. My father never threw punches at me but backing away, bobbing and weaving, let me flail, as he shouted hands up, snap that jab, now the right, one two, that's it, you're telegraphing your punches, try the body, your head is open, on your toes. I took some pride in my left hook, though his right was always there to catch it. I would jab two or three times, then dip and follow a jab with the hook, my weight on my left foot, pushing off from the right foot. Sometimes my hook would land with enough force to push his glove into his face or ear. That was as close as I came to doing any damage. We talked boxing all the time, and we took in the fights at the Olympic and the Hollywood Legion Stadium. My father told me of the great fights he had seen and had been in, how a fellow hired to stage a fight with him in a picture had got smart and landed a couple, and my father had decked him in seconds with a fast combination. They printed it, and he had a lot of laughs later when people asked why the fight looked so real. I found myself dreaming of the ring. The hook would land and my father would go down.

But at school each morning I was so exhausted that I confused King Cheops with Queen Hatshepsut, I could scarcely parse a sentence, and the baseball coach inquired whether I had taken to self-abuse or was staying out all night with girls. I wanted to protest to my father that I was not yet half the man he thought I was, but as I flagged, he flourished. In a couple of months he would bring in Marshall Marshall, who was a pretty fair heavyweight, and give him the surprise of his life, because a quick little man could beat a slow big man. Look what happened to Primo Carnera.

One morning he woke me half an hour earlier than usual. It wasn't the hallucinations. Our workouts had routed them.

'Rise and shine, Salty. I've got something special for you. Wash the old face and brush the old hair, and don't forget to dry between your toes. Keeps away the jungle rot.'

When I had done these things, he sat me down, brought me a cup of java, and told me to shut my eyes. Into my hands he placed a package wrapped in saved string and torn paper bags, inscribed in letters that had been gone over several times in pencil and in ink, 'To My Son, Salty, Always a Champion in my Book, From His Dad, Papa-san.' Inside was a pair of boxing trunks, shiny white, with black stripes down the sides. I thanked him, and he said I could wear them this morning if I liked, because a champion ought to dress like a champion. I closed myself in the bathroom and put them on over a jock-strap he had given me for Christmas. They were much too large. The elastic waistband hardly touched me, and they smelled of mothballs. I emerged, holding up the trunks with both hands, and my father said that they looked terrific. Now I could whip anybody. I reminded him of himself when he had been light-heavyweight champ of the Pacific Fleet during the twilight hours of World War I. He had been sixteen then. He had lied about his age because he had wanted to see the world. I probably hadn't realized it, but these trunks I had on had been his own, and now he wanted me to have them. No, not the ones he had had in the Navy, they were long gone. These had been given to him in 1930 by Blackie O'Donough, a scrappy middleweight from San Francisco, who wrote poetry and ran a café in Ferndale which we had to visit sometime.

'I wore them in a fight picture I made that year, *Northside-Southside*. I played a guy from the wrong side of the tracks. You know the story. I turn down a fix and beat the bejesus out of a punk backed by the Syndicate. You can wear the trunks this morning, Salty, at the Club. Wait till Vic sees you.'

When I suggested that they would not stay up, he said I could wear them with a belt, no one would notice. I said that I could not wear them, much as I appreciated the gift. I would never fit into them. I was smaller than he was and I always would be smaller. There was another thing. I could not go on with the morning routine. It was killing me.

He was hurt. He looked like he had been hit by Dempsey. He couldn't understand me. He wanted me to avoid some of the mistakes he had made. He wanted me to be happy. Whatever I wanted.

'It's your life, Salty.'

Then he wanted to know whether I still had Preacher Roe's mitt. Did I remember the day Chuck Connors gave it to me? That had been a hell of a day.

'Sure I still have it,' I said. 'I use it every day. I keep it at school.'

'That was a great day,' he said. 'I was real proud of you. I could see that Chuck Connors could recognize a talent. You keep it oiled up, don't you?'

'Sure I do.'

'I think I have a can of neatsfoot oil some place,' he said, 'if you need it. You want to take good care of a thing like that. We had some great times, didn't we? I guess you could say I was a pretty fair father, couldn't you?'

'You sure could,' I said.

He continued to visit the Club on his own. He saw Ford occasionally, and Marshall Marshall. With the good weather he was at the beach, and once a week he had lunch with his confessor. I suspect they talked about me, because I had begun to miss mass, and I never went to confession any more. The priests had nothing to tell me, and I did not wish to reveal to them the lusts and devious schemes of one who felt himself a prisoner. I was trapped in a fantasy dungeon, fed memories and lies. My jailer had forgotten what I was in for but he wanted to keep me there for company, and he liked to try experiments on me, dress me in funny clothes, see what I could take. Thinking over the boxing, I compared myself to the Jews the Germans froze half to death to see if they could fuck themselves to life again. There was also the example of Serbo-Croatian children raised in boxes so they would emerge suitably crooked, worth tossing pennies at. If I were sprung, he would be out of business for good. But there was nobody out there to spring me. Certainly I could not count on my sot of a mother. She acted only for a price, and I had nothing to pay her. I could count on myself. I was getting ready to make my break. I would try to get away unnoticed.

EIGHTEEN

Loss

There grew up between us long silences, when I would read and he would stare at the wall or thumb through his correspondence and say that it was a sign of real friendship when two fellows didn't feel they had to say anything to each other. Or we would have words about how often I was going out and when I was coming home. 'It's your life' became his standard dictum, as though he regretted I was shooting horse but did not wish to interfere. I knew he wanted to rescue me, to be my hero, to appear at the police station at four in the morning and get me released in his custody, to pay off some father threatening a paternity suit, but he was frustrated, I stayed out of trouble, there was less and less he could do for me, except when I caught the flu. He intercepted all incoming calls, reported my temperature, and said that I was too weak to come to the phone. He had no idea when I would recover, it might take weeks. I got well as quickly as possible.

Then came the telegram from Donna Esmeralda Cordova announcing my mother's death. The official cause was heart. I imagined that she had collapsed among the shrimp shells on the floor of a bar in Madrid, but Donna Esmeralda simply reported a collapse, and we never learned more. Mother had left her securities to Donna Esmeralda, whose husband the duke had fallen on hard times, and her body to science. My father pleaded with the American consul over the telephone, but it was too late, she had already been carved up. How often he must have wished her dead! Now that wish too had been taken away. He had purchased a family plot. He had planned to lie with her there forever; I could be tossed in later; he would get us both, eventually. All he could do now was to arrange a mass for the repose of her soul.

Leave her alone, I thought, leave her be, leave her in pieces, you are never going to put her back together, she has been gone for years. In death she appeared to me as she had not for so long, scented, smiling, East Seventies elegant. We were planning another party. We were choosing her husband. I was staying home from school to be with her one day, and we were driving out to Casa Fiesta, looking at it through binoculars from the road, wondering what the new owners were like, and we were driving on, saying it was a new life now, the two of us, our Malibu picnic, seashore sandwiches, secret love bonds laughter-promised. She did make me feel grown up. I did watch the men wanting her. I had come to wish her dead, that was something I would not escape, I was another imperfect man wanting to kill her, but she had fooled us all, she had just left. Nothing now to want from her or for her. Dead mother, drunk mother, dead mother, wrecked mother, dead mother, poor mother.

'We'll pray for her,' my father said. 'These things can do a lot of good. You never can tell.'

'I'm not going,' I said.

'This is no time,' he said. 'She was still a young woman. God will take that into account. We owe her to make every effort.'

I felt I owed her nothing, or that I had nothing to owe her but reproaches tangled in shames tangled in regrets, and I wasn't believing in God any more anyway, but looking at him, his worry-beaten hulk, I knew that it was no time for an adolescent-rejection-confrontation scene. He needed the mass and me with him, to make sense of these lives and this death. So what if I didn't believe? So what if the mass was a little victory for him over her, over me? To say no to him now would be a kick square in his battered old balls. My university tuition was coming due. I would watch my step.

Dad told the priest about how Mother had lain in state in the Spanish cathedral and about the condolences he had received from Generalissimo Franco. An announcement was placed in the parish bulletin, but there were only the two of us and the usual eight o'clock weekday mass old women. We knelt front row center, stayed kneeling or standing throughout. My father must have thought she was hanging onto purgatory by her fingernails and that if we sat down, she would plunge forever. He forbore even to rest his ass against the pew's edge, but I took that much risk. I thought of her and all her lovers, wondered which of them were loves, knew that none of them had matched the mad devotion of the lover kneeling next to me, knew that I had not, willed to love her more now, put my head down on my arms hoping that this weight I felt on me, this emptiness I felt in me, meant that I loved her.

'Trust in God, son, trust in God,' my father whispered to me. 'Without faith in this life you got nothing.'

I believe in God the Father Almighty, Creator of heaven and earth. And Christ don't forget the Virgin Mary. And the Catholic Church. And how about the U.S. Navy? And Admiral Jack Ford. And your brother who stole your money. And Marshall Marshall who trusts in you who trusted her whose death we celebrate today. Sam Caliban where are you when I need you write me a check I want to take a plane to the promised land, Palm Springs will do. Maybe she wasn't so bad after all. Maybe she was looking for somebody who wasn't such a trusting shining asshole that was ready to believe anything even from her. Holy Jesus I vowed then that I would not go through life trusting. She knew she was a liar and she knew he was a liar too. How could she believe in a liar who believed in her? I knew my father was praying for me right then and I did not want his prayers, they oppressed me, they drained the blood from me. She would not want them either, ghoul prayers, knife-prayers cutting. I was lying on the dissecting table with her being cut by the knives of his prayers. If I could take his knives and cut him back. I pray to God that all your members be blistered and covered with sores. May your fore-skin grow an ulcer. Shit, he had taken enough shit. The mass was interminable. By the end of it I was nobody, nothing but a collection of losses, lies, hates, evasions, dying to escape, to steal an identity, become a Spaniard and go kill Donna Es-meralda and her duke and take my money to Argentina.

At home my father discoursed on the value of religion and on the free doughnuts and coffee we had received after mass. It was things like that that made the church a friendly place and not something to be afraid of. I avoided religion and told him of my plans. I needed to go East well before the term began be-cause I was behind in my reading and there would be stiff competition from the Eastern prep school boys who had been reading Aristotle from the cradle. It was like preparing for a big game. I had to be in tip-top mental condition. I needed to get cracking in the university library. I didn't know who my opponents would be, but I couldn't be caught off guard, they would be gunning for me from behind every bookshelf. I had to fight for my place. I almost convinced myself. Maybe I would convince myself. I might get somewhere, besides just out.

'I get it,' he said. 'Maybe this is the time. I've been saving something for you, and there are some things I want you to know about. You know, you might come back here some time and find the old man dead. It happens.'

He showed me where he kept the extra keys to the house and car, just in case. I wouldn't have to worry about burial ex-penses. He would get rid of the family plot somehow, there must be other people who could use the space.

'It was a nice idea, wasn't it?' he asked. 'All of us together again some day?'

'It was,' I said. Too bad, I thought, he had not had the

Christian charity to include Anatol. And who knew how many holes I might require, by the time I was through fucking up?

But some things weren't meant to be, he went on, and he had always wanted to be buried at sea anyway. The Navy had a deal. They would ship him out of San Diego and drop him over the side.

'You aren't sick, are you?' I asked.

'No, but these things can hit you, and you can't be too prepared. I don't want to be any expense to you. It won't cost a thing. I do want the Catholic burial service. I do want that, if you could make sure I get that.'

'Of course.'

'Well that's taken care of. Now follow me.'

He led me out to the garage where the saddle was and a lot of boxes we had never gone through. I was afraid he was going to confront me with the rest of Linda's letters and I readied a speech: at least I had known what it was to have a girl and it wouldn't be the last and I did not intend to spend the rest of my life beating off over old photographs of my perfidious wife who was resting in a Spanish garbage can now anyway. But he ignored the saddle and pulled a big plastic bag out of a box. We went back into the house and he put the bag in the middle of the floor and stood over it. I sat down.

'I've been keeping this for you,' he said. 'My father did the same for me. He used to ask me for money when I was in the chips, and then when he died I discovered he had been putting it all away for me. There was fifty thousand dollars. Well, I'm afraid I can't match that, though I know you're counting on me for your tuition, and I wouldn't deny my son that, because he didn't get a scholarship.'

'I explained that,' I said, a little testy. 'I couldn't get a scholarship because you have too much money.'

'I'll borrow it somewhere, Salty. What I have here is for you gratis. It's a start for you, no strings attached, and I know you'll do the right thing with it.'

Out of the big plastic bag he pulled a brown paper bag, and another paper bag out of that, and another paper bag, and finally a canvas bag that went chink, when he set it down.

'Your grandmother left this for you,' he said. 'This is your inheritance from her. She didn't leave anything to anyone else, not even to me, even though I took care of her when your mother wouldn't, her own daughter, and I had her on the payroll in the old days, as a secretary. That got her the social security. But this is yours. She was very fond of you, Salty.'

I must have misjudged her. A gift from beyond the grave. Hello. What a pleasant surprise. Do come in. You're dropping charcoal on the carpet. I took the bag. It was heavy. I looked in. It was full of silver dollars, fifty or sixty of them. I stuck my hand in and fingered and jingled them. But why had he kept them from me? Could I take him to court? He owed me interest. I plunged down to the bottom of the bag and my fingers touched something soft.

'What's this?' I said. I pulled out a little leather change purse.

'I don't know,' my father said. 'Let me see that.'

I handed him the purse, automatically, and immediately I wanted to snatch it back. He looked at it and held it up without opening it. He must have looked into the bag and seen the silver dollars, but he had never noticed the purse. I could see he was a little anxious. He wanted to open the purse but he did not know whether he wanted me to see what was inside, whatever it was. I was not going to let that purse out of my sight. And I was going to keep whatever was inside it. I calculated how quickly I could reach the six-gun under his bed. If he wanted a showdown, I would give it to him.

'Open it,' I said.

'I am,' he said. He turned his back to me.

I got up to look over his shoulder. He opened the purse and we looked in. There was a small wad of pink toilet paper in it. He picked out the wad and held it up. Through a hole in the paper I caught a glint of metal. So did he. He went over to the table and bent over the wad.

'What is it,' I said, 'cufflinks?'

'That's right,' he said. 'Cufflinks. It's my cufflinks.'

'What cufflinks? What are they doing in there?'

He said nothing. I had him cornered. I got around to where I could see. He had to unwrap the thing now. It was a diamond ring.

'That's mine,' I said, and I took it from him. He had no ad-lib and let it go without a struggle.

'I'm very touched,' I said. 'She promised it to me. It's her engagement ring. I asked her to marry me when I was about ten and she promised me this ring. I'm really touched.' I pocketed it.

In my mind I was already making a raid on Brooks Brothers. I had seen pictures of the undergraduates at my university and I didn't dress anything like them. Now I would not have to arrive looking like some California cowboy. I would go to New York, stay at the Plaza, open a charge at Brooks and arrive on campus a vision in tweed. It would be my first step toward being more like everybody else. I was bibulous with hope. Good-bye now, good-bye. I'll be seeing you. I'm jumping ship. You'll hear from me airmail. I'll clue you in on what I'm learning, keep you posted on my career, let you know if I get elected President, and one day we'll sit around and reminisce about the great old times gone by, the golden days, the never to be forgotten glamor of it all. So long, Marshall Marshall, may you live to sell MacArthur for a million. A tip of the hat to you, dear mother of mine, there's a flower blooming from your offal somewhere in old Madrid, may a sailor pick it for his sweetheart. And a thousand thanks to you, Granny, fan I never knew, I've got a piece of you here in my pocket, the only piece that didn't burn. By authority vested in me by nobody, I posthumously promote you, whatever rank you wish, just name it, I'll never mistrust a Methodist again.

And as for you, Linda, you'll never go shoeless, but don't count me out yet, baby, I haven't begun to fight. The time will come you'll wish you'd given your big ignorant jock the old heave-ho.

'A ring like that might be worth a couple of thousand,' my father said. 'She promised it to you, is that it?'

I took it out and held it to the light. It was a good-sized rock all right.

'I wouldn't want to sell it,' I said, making it snug again, my fist guarding the flap. 'Not unless I had to. A gift like that. It's a family link.'

'What you ought to do,' my father said, 'is let me put it in the safety deposit box for you. You might want to give it to the mother of your children. You might not. It'd be there when you need it.'

'No,' I said.

'A safety deposit box is the place for a thing like that.'

'No it isn't,' I said. He was down, and as we looked at each other there were thousands of miles between us, but in a second I realized he was not out, not yet. If he suspected that I was going to sell the ring, if he found out that I had sold it, I could expect to find the bill for my tuition right in my lap.

'I tell you what,' I said. 'The safety deposit box is probably a good idea. You have more experience with things like this than I do. The first thing I'll do when I get East is find a bank and put the ring in a safety deposit box. That way it'll be safe.'

'Now you're talking,' he said.

I did not know whether he knew that he had been out-maneuvered. I did not know whether he knew, whether he could face the fact, that had he discovered the ring by himself, I would never have seen it; that had Granny not had his number, so she knew enough not to tell him about it and to hide it from him, I would never have seen it; that he would have told himself, was telling himself right then, that he needed it, deserved it more than I did because he had paid Granny's social security and had taken care of her until she died when her own daughter wouldn't; that the silver dollars he had hidden from me for over two years would alone have been enough to present to me as a grand self-sacrificing generous gesture of paternal love and regard for this boy who was going off needing to remember that his old Dad was one hell of a guy who wished him well in whatever he did. I did guess that he knew very little about me, and for once, at last, I was glad of that. Just stick with me, son. Stick with me and someday you might get part of your inheritance from your grandmother. He was trusting, all right. He trusted me not to know his treachery.

'Look at the way things turn out,' my father said. 'This morning we were remembering your mother and praying for her, and now you have this good luck. I'm happy for you, I really am.'

He opened his arms and I went into them, and he gave me a big bear hug. Trust. Faith. He had tried everything to hang onto me. If he had known what he was hugging he would not have held so tight. Cut! The scene was overplayed. Dissolve, dissolve, bring the music up. We're busting hell out of the budget, boys. He released me. I saw his eyes watering and I let my eyes go out of focus. He said:

'I offered up a prayer for you this morning. I always do. And I thought of something my father often said to me. He told me it one time when I was in some hot water and I thought the whole world was against me. He said to me, "Son," he said, "son, just remember this. Right or wrong, I'm behind you. Right or wrong, I'm your father and pal." Your father and pal. I think that's pretty good, don't you? And Salty, I say it to you tonight. Right or wrong, I'm your father and pal. And I wish you all the luck in the world, believe me. How's that? How's that from a father to a son?'

I went into the world well-armed.

—Dublin, *S.S. Eurybates*, Claremont, 1973–1976